Witches of Westridge

Westridge Cove Mystery Series
Book 1

J.L. Hyde

First paperback edition March 2026

Cover Design by Allsweet Studios and Brandon Kobs

ISBN 979-8-9871631-7-7

(Paperback)

www.jlhyde.com

 Formatted with Vellum

Also by J.L. Hyde:

Underground

Delta County

Summer of '99

Midnight in Delta County

Magnolia Court

Grady Lake

Secrets of Grady

Ghosts of Grady

The Bluff

To All Those I've Killed Before

For Alfonz,
Finishing this book while buried deep in grief from losing
you almost got the best of me, but I powered through, and it
reminded me: We can do hard things.
This one's for you.

Author's Note

The Westridge Cove Mystery Series is told in three parts, and this book serves as Part One. While many of your questions will be answered by the end of this volume, other elements of the story will be resolved in the final two installments.
I hope you come to love these characters as much as I do as you make your way through the story.
Readers, welcome to Westridge Cove.

Prologue

The man from the bar is chasing me.

I knew he had bad intentions from the moment he walked into the musty dive and stared at my chest like it was a freshly cooked ribeye. He didn't *ask* if he could buy me a drink; he *told* me he was going to. He leaned against the curved wooden railing of the bar and shouted an order to the bartender, without a hint of please or thank you. He kept his back to me so I wouldn't see what he was slipping into my bourbon and cranberry, mixing it quickly with a black stir straw before turning to hand it to me. Throughout the night, his hands unnecessarily grazed my arm or waist each time he told another story that I couldn't possibly be less interested in. Oh yes; the red flags were aplenty.

Reluctantly, I told him about my passion for pro football when he asked about my hobbies, which inevitably led to a pop quiz about random stats to prove I'm a fan, as men tend to do when a woman dares to show interest in their sacred sport.

"Ah, an NFL fan? Do you know who won the Super Bowl last year, or were you just watching it for the commercials, sweetheart?"

Breathe. Don't react with emotion.

"I made a killing on that game because I nailed every leg of my parlay. The guys at work thought I was nuts to take Philly, but I was the only one to come out ahead that weekend."

I wasn't sure why I entertained his idiotic, chauvinistic line of questioning. Maybe I was playing a game with myself to see how repulsed I could possibly get by this man. By his third not-so-subtle crotch adjustment, I reached my limit.

Whilst in the middle of his football interrogation, I realized my friend Lucy had been in the bathroom for over ten minutes. She either had food poisoning from the questionable sushi she ate against my advice, or she ran into someone she knew and was currently locked in a conversation. With her sensitive stomach and inability to shut the fuck up, it was a toss-up, really.

"Wow, okay. So you watched the big game," he answered, both hands held up in defense before one dropped for yet another itch of the crotch. *What did he have going on down there?* "Alright, who is your favorite Heisman winner of all time?"

I watched him lean his dumb elbow on the pub table between us, but before I could lay into him about how I was sick of this test—my answer would have been Charles Woodson, closely followed by Baker Mayfield because I like his tenacity—Lucy slithered in behind me and wrapped an arm around my waist.

"Is he trying to test your football knowledge? Oh, boy."

Lucy leaned her chin on my shoulder, staring at Chad and daring him to continue his line of questioning.

"Look, I love football. It's definitely in my top two favorite hobbies," I confirmed.

"What's the second hobby?" he asked, head cocked, and staring straight at me like Lucy didn't exist.

"Oh, that's not something I disclose so soon after meeting someone."

Lucy threw her head back and cackled at my response.

This further piqued his interest, as Lucy knew it would. That rotten little instigator.

"Anyway," she said only to me, purposely icing him out, "I ate something that didn't agree with me, so I'm going to head back to the apartment. Can you survive on your own?"

I nodded and gave her a wink. She shook her head as she walked away. She's never had to worry about me before. Why would tonight be any different?

And fucking look at me now.

I am running for my life in the wooded lot behind Charlie's Bar that this city recently rezoned as a disc golf course for some damn reason. It's not that I have any particular vendetta against the sport, but right now it's creating a whole lot of wide-open spaces where I need cover.

I had a feeling he wasn't going to let me go easy after asking where I live twice (*I don't give my address to strangers, Chad*), telling me I'd had too much to drink to make it home alone (*I've only had two cocktails, Chad*), and repeatedly insisting that he's one of the good guys (*I'm sure you are, Chad*).

When he finally left the bar, seemingly deflated from the rejection, I watched through the tiny porthole window next to the unoccupied booth in the front corner of the bar. Sure enough, he walked to his car, looked around a few times, and then slipped into the unlit alley between the hardware store and Mauve's Salon and Taxidermy—that business combination being a story for another day.

Foolishly, I questioned whether he may be trying to find another bar for a night cap at the other end of the alley. Maybe one with some intoxicated females who were far easier to manipulate. Like playing the slots—this one's not giving me any love; I'd better cash out and move on down to something shinier. This thought also made me uneasy, because who would be there to protect another girl from this creep?

I barely made it a block from the bar when I heard the footsteps approaching behind me. I was right; he was waiting for me. When I swung around and saw his beady black eyes and emotionless expression, I knew not to stick around long enough to inquire about this man's intentions. He had at least fifty pounds and six inches on me, and the chances of overpowering him were slim to none, so I did what would result in my best chance of survival: I ran.

It's not lost on me that I'm currently running in the opposite direction of any residential areas— you know, the ones with homes that have people inside who could actually hear my screams and call the authorities. Nobody really knows how they'll react when put in a situation like this. The mind makes strange decisions when your body is juiced with adrenaline and time is limited. Until you're put in a fight-or-flight situation, you have no idea what your reaction to such an immediate and immense threat will be. The only reason I had the good sense to run is because I've been over this scenario in my head many, many times.

I know there's a thick patch of trees on the opposite side of this clearing. It backs up to the cliffs that sit atop the lake. If I can just make it over there, I can hide behind one of the thick tree trunks I saw this morning on my dumb little mental health walk. On a side note, my therapist has requested that I stop referring to them as "dumb little mental health walks," but I have no interest in complying with that request. I have yet to comply with *a lot* of requests that old bird makes, but I show up every two weeks and that's gotta count for something.

One piece of knowledge comforts me: The predator chasing me is not a local. He doesn't know these woods like I do, so there's no way he can navigate them in the dark as well as I can. He goes to college here. This is simply a four-year temporary home for him, but it's practically my backyard, just one town over from where I was born and raised. Finding an adequate hiding spot gives me a fighting chance at winning this battle.

I don't waste the time to stop and listen for his boots crunching on the freshly fallen leaves—I sprint toward my destination without looking back. My feet are hitting the ground so violently, I worry that I'll slip on the wet grass from this afternoon's rain. My breaths are becoming haggard, and I wonder if I should have ran cross country with my friends when they offered, instead of mocking their exercise habits with a powdered donut in each hand. I could have built up some stamina for an occasion such as this.

Luck is on my side as I slide into the wooded area on the far end of the course and immediately find a fallen tree with a trunk thick enough to conceal my sweaty, panting body. I dive behind it. I will my breathing to slow so he won't hear it in the quiet night. After a few deep inhales to steady my pulse, the sound of the waves lapping on the shoreline below is all that I hear. I close my eyes to focus on detecting noise from any crunching leaves, so I can tell which direction he's coming from. I know he saw me sprint across the clearing, so it's only a matter of time before he gets close to my hiding spot. I need to be ready.

I feel something crawling up my neck and it takes everything in me not to squeal. I tell myself it's a butterfly and most definitely not a wood spider. Just a beautiful little monarch awakened in its sleep on this beautiful September night. I'm not even sure where butterflies sleep or if they've already migrated south for the year, but this lie seems to de-escalate my impending panic, so I stick with it.

I stiffen at the sound of a broken twig at the entrance to the woods.

I hear him whisper, "Ashley . . . Aaaashleeeey. Just come out, sweetheart. Let's talk."

One more step and it's closer this time.

As slow and controlled as I possibly can, I inhale. Hold for four seconds. Exhale. I take back half of what I said about this new therapist; her advice is good for something. I feel my back pocket for the folded note I slid in there earlier. Still there.

He pauses at a tree, and I hear his hand grabbing at the bark to steady himself. This fool is as out of shape as I am.

Trying to catch his breath, he slowly walks a few more steps. He must be dragging his feet because the sound I'm hearing is of leaves being scattered rather than stepped on.

Two more steps in my direction.

I check my watch.

Thud.

I gasp and peek over the fallen tree between us.

He's dropped to his knees, less than ten feet away.

I smile.

This is my favorite part, and it's happening two and a half minutes earlier than I'd expected. I'm going to need to get this timing down before the next one.

Slapping away the unidentified insect, which has now made its way to my shoulder, I quickly climb to my feet, dust the dirt and leaves off my behind, and walk toward him.

"What's . . . what's happening?" he asks, his chin bobbing forward a few times before he finally gives in and leans toward the ground, his hands catching him at the last moment before his face smacks the forest floor.

"What's happening, Chad? Well, I'd love to tell you. You see, we've been following you for months. You've been up to no good, haven't you, Chad?" I *tsk* a few times while he struggles to keep his eyes open and focused on me. "You know that drug you slipped into my cocktail tonight—the one I pretended to drink but dumped into the fake plastic ficus tree? Well, I slipped something a whole lot stronger into yours when you went to the bathroom to handle whatever the hell you've got going on in your pants. It's time for *you* to find out how it feels to be powerless, my dude."

This is when the panic sets in. He tries to fight it.

"Not so fun being the victim, now is it?" I add.

He may be bigger and stronger than me, but modern medicine works wonders at evening the playing field.

"Ashley . . . we . . . we can talk," he whispers, trailing off.

I turn my head when I sense movement at the entrance to our secluded wooded spot.

"I see you've discovered her other hobby, Chad," Lucy says, leaning forward to pat his head like a dog.

"I might even enjoy this more than football."

"Ashley . . . please," he manages to say.

"Oh, my name isn't Ashley," I respond, leaning down to Chad's level. I grab his chin, jerking his head up and forcing him to look me in the eyes. "You may not be from around here, but I'm certain you've heard my name before."

Slowly, I lean forward and whisper it in his ear.

Despite the drugs pumping through his veins to sedate his entire system, Chad's eyes grow wide at my words, and he whips his head back before screaming into the night.

It seems like an evil-villain move to laugh at his pain, but damn if I can't help cackling.

Chapter One

OCTOBER 27TH, 1993

"**I**'ve heard this new cereal is *da bomb*," Peter Thornwick said with raised eyebrows as he set the skinny blue box in front of his daughter. "It's like Rice Crispies Treats . . . but in a cereal."

"Dad, please don't ever say that again," Sarah said as she entered the kitchen, grabbed a banana from the fruit bowl, and put her Walkman headphones on before leaving out the back door. She waited to hit play until she got outside, lest she hear her parents complain about her "dark taste in music" again.

"What, what did I say?" he asked, turning to his wife.

"These kids don't want us using their slang, dear," Sheila Thornwick told him with a kiss on the temple. "It's because we're old."

"Who are you calling old?" he asked.

"I think they look great, Dad," Margaret said, pulling the box close and opening it. "I can't wait to try them."

"Four daughters and only one of them has turned out to

be a sweetheart," he told Margaret—his little Maggie—leaning across the breakfast bar to pinch her nose. "You're my youngest and my only hope, kid."

Maggie smiled and watched as her father turned to stare out the small window over the kitchen sink. The leaves were beginning to fall like orange and yellow snowflakes, littering the yard of their split-level home. Where the girls and their mother saw beauty, her father only saw work.

"What a week for a work shutdown. I'm never going to have the time to take care of these damn leaves," he muttered to nobody in particular.

"Peter. Language," Sheila reminded him, nodding toward their youngest daughter.

"It's okay, Mom. I hear a lot worse at school."

Sheila gasped. "What? From whom?"

Their attention was quickly stolen by a light thud from two Converse sneakers landing at the bottom of the stairs, followed by shuffled footsteps into the kitchen.

"Nobody's swearing at school, Mom. Maggie's kidding. It's nothing but the Lord's Prayer, casserole recipes, and book club discussions, I assure you."

"Don't patronize me, Bridget."

Bridget shrugged before sliding onto the stool next to her sister and briefly studying the new cereal box before pouring herself a bowl. "These are da bomb, Dad," she said with a mouthful.

"Hah! I told you!"

Bridget winked at her mother, who couldn't help but smile. Sheila finished packing a second ham and cheese sandwich into her husband's blue tin lunch box, alongside an apple, brownie, can of pop, and bag of chips. Placing her hand flat on top and pushing forcefully, she struggled to close the lid. Peter noticed this and took it from her hands, pushing down on the lid with a little heft until he heard the latches catch.

"Two sandwiches? Is it shutdown week?" Bridget asked.

"You betcha. Get a good look at this handsome face because you won't be seeing much of it until after Halloween."

"You know we appreciate you, right, Dad?" Maggie asked, setting her spoon down on the edge of the bowl.

Before he could make another joke about his youngest daughter being the sweetest, Bridget added, "We all do. We love you."

He'd made a lot of mistakes in his life, but he'd somehow managed to do something right with these girls. He dreamed for years of having a son so he could watch the Packers play ball and share an ice-cold beer when he was of age, but now Peter couldn't imagine a life without his four daughters. The eldest, Nancy, had a daughter of her own now, but she still made time to stop by on Sundays and cheer on the green and gold with her old man. She even brings a six-pack of cold ones with her most weeks—who needs a son, right?

As of September, the girls who remained living at home were all in high school. If it weren't for the ridiculous hours he spent working at the paper mill in town, he'd be sitting at home with a shotgun, worried sick about his three beautiful daughters. Although they had wildly different personalities, they'd all inherited their mother's long, thick, and wavy brunette hair and dark brown eyes. They'd always turn a lot of heads on family vacation, with fellow husbands usually giving Peter a sympathetic shake of the head. *Better him than me,* they would think. How can one man ensure the safety of five beautiful women, all bearing his last name? He'd decided a long time ago that his best course of action was to prepare the girls to be out on their own because he couldn't watch all of them all the time.

So far, he was o for 1. His oldest, Nancy, was a single mother in her early twenties, who seemed satisfied cleaning houses for the elite of Westridge Cove and wouldn't even tell him or Sheila who the father of little Iris could be. He could only hope his remaining three would use more discernment when choosing a man to spend their lives with. Or a woman. It was the nineties, after all. Nancy most certainly chose the wrong man because what kind of guy would leave an eighteen-year-old pregnant and alone? He'll never forget watching Nancy walk across the stage at graduation, her gown draped over her slightly protruding belly. It's not how they envisioned their eldest daughter entering the real world, but he and Sheila quickly adapted and couldn't be more thrilled to be grandparents. Luckily, Nancy's daughter, Iris, just turned six and is adjusting just fine to being raised by a single mother. It's no doubt that having three aunts and two grandparents who love her dearly has also helped.

"I love you girls, too. And enjoy this peace and quiet while it lasts because I have fifteen more years until retirement, and I plan to spend the majority of my time driving you all nuts. Especially you," Peter said, wrapping his arm around his wife's waist and pulling her in for a kiss.

"You drive me nuts now, dear," Sheila responded, before leaning forward into a hug while he cocooned his thick arms around her shoulders.

"Yuck, get a room, guys," Bridget said, her nose scrunching in disgust.

"Don't roll your eyes too hard—they'll get stuck that way," her dad joked as he pulled his work jacket off the hook next to the back door. "Okay, girls, have fun babysitting tonight, and don't let those kids watch any spooky movies or they'll be up with nightmares all night long, and you'll be hearing from their parents."

"Ann's mom said that Westridge Rentals got the demo tape for *Hocus Pocus* early and she's going to let us borrow it. It's a Disney movie; the kids will love it," Margaret tells him.

"An advance copy? You girls be sure to thank Mrs. Haven for letting you borrow it. She's a busy woman running that place and it's awfully nice of her to go out of her way for you. And make sure it's okay with the Carters that you use their VCR. And make sure you rewind it before you give it back. Will Ann be stopping by?"

"Yeah, she's going to help us because we have Iris tonight, too," Bridget said, immediately regretting the words when she saw both of her parents jerk slightly in response.

The three youngest Thornwick sisters had formed an unofficial babysitter's club, and their older sister Nancy loved to drop her daughter off with them so she could have a night out with her friends. Best of all, it was in her price range—free. The sisters didn't mind it; they loved Iris and they all agreed that Nancy deserved a night off once in a while. Their parents disagreed and felt that Nancy was taking advantage of her little sisters and not putting the interests of her daughter first.

"That's the third time this month. What in the hell is Nancy doing, hanging out at the bars? And with what money?" Peter asked as he opened the door. "I've got to go to work, but I'll be talking to her about her responsibilities as a parent when she comes over on Sunday. I'll tell you what your mother and I were doing when we had you girls: We were sitting our butts at home and facing the music.

That's what we signed up for when we decided to have children."

The door closed with a little more force than usual, which was about as close to having a temper that Peter Thornwick was capable of. As the girls' friends liked to say, Mr. Thornwick was like a TV dad: dumb jokes, zero temper, working all the time, loves his family. Much like Clark W. Griswold, he may have been one of the last true family men.

"Give me the dirt, girls. Where is your sister going?" Sheila asked her daughters in a hushed tone the minute she heard the engine to Peter's pickup truck roar to life.

Maggie and Bridget shared a look and then a shrug as they decided in unison that they were going to rat their sister out. It's what little sisters do. Plus, they couldn't stand keeping secrets from their mom.

"She's going to the Nirvana concert in Kalamazoo," Margaret said, turning to Bridget to see if she wanted to add any more detail to the confession.

"With whom?" Sheila asked, eyes darting between the girls.

"A friend she met," Bridget offered.

"Is this friend a boy?"

Neither girl answered.

"So your sister is driving down to Kalamazoo on a Wednesday night to watch some sort of rock band with a boy she just met and is leaving her six-year-old daughter with you?"

That was the moment the girls regretted divulging the information to their mother. Nancy would kill them when she found out.

Chapter Two

OCTOBER 27TH, 1993

By the time the final bell rang at Westridge High, autumn leaves were blowing across the streets of the small northern town like mini tumbleweeds. The wind speeds had increased to such a level that the lake freighters had to seek shelter in the bay to protect themselves from the harsh gusts and massive waves surging around them. The gales of November had arrived early.

The Thornwick sisters each made their way home from school separately, with plans to leave for the Carters' at five o'clock sharp, so they could make the ten-minute walk and arrive with plenty of time to be briefed by the parents before they left for the night. The girls were watching five children in total—their niece, Iris (unpaid, of course), the two Carter boys, and two of the neighbors' kids, the DeYoung boys. None of the children were younger than six, so it would be an easy money night. No diapers, no bottles, and hopefully no crying.

Maggie, the youngest of the Thornwicks, began the six-block walk home alongside her lab partner, Jessa. The entirety of their commute was spent talking about the new boy who just transferred in from downstate. He had braces and a bad case of chin acne, but both girls saw potential. They planned to befriend him the next day at lunch so they could get in on the ground floor when he emerged junior year with straight teeth and pristine skin. It was an investment in their future social statuses.

Bridget, newly sixteen, rode her bike home solo while fantasizing about owning every Pontiac Grand Am or Firebird that passed on her route. She couldn't wait to have wheels. By her calculation, she'd only have to pick up about forty-eight more babysitting shifts before she'd have enough for a downpayment. She'd already picked out the fuzzy steering wheel cover she planned to purchase at Shopko, and the first CD she'd play while pulling into the parking lot of Westridge High: *Very Necessary* by Salt-N-Pepa. She may be a tragically white, unhip teenager from the Upper Peninsula of Michigan, but when she was alone in her room, she could rap along with every single lyric to *Shoop* and *Whatta Man*. But if one of the popular boys asked for a ride home from school, she'd put in The Cure or The Black Crowes so she'd seem cooler than she really was. If they said, "nice music," she'd shrug and turn it up. Effortlessly cool; that's what she'd be when she owned a car.

Although she was officially an adult at eighteen years old, Sarah Thornwick certainly didn't feel like one. She had a fear of getting behind the wheel; she'd barely lasted a full day in driver's ed before dropping out. She shook Mr. Leonoff's hand as she gathered her belongings, like they'd completed a business deal. *Thanks for all the parallel parking tips, but this gig just ain't for me, sir.* She had yet to apply to any colleges and tuned her dad out any time he tried to educate her on paying taxes or getting an apartment. She liked her life just the way it was—simple, easy, and paid for. Every dollar she made from her babysitting gigs went into a savings account at Northern Michigan Credit Union for a yet-to-be-determined future. She'd figure out a plan someday, but it sure wouldn't be today.

"Did you apply to State?" her friend Noelle asked as they zipped their backpacks and twisted the dials to secure their lockers, pulling to test them in unison.

"I'm not trying to live in East Lansing," Sarah responded, slinging her bag over her left shoulder. "That's like six hours away."

"You know, most people eventually move away from their parents. At least for a few years."

"It's not my parents I'm worried about leaving. It's Iris. She needs me."

Noelle wanted to remind Sarah that most people also leave their nieces to go to college, but she respected the dedication her friend had when it came to helping her sister raise Iris. All three Thornwick girls had been in that little girl's life since the moment she was born. Her father may not be in the picture, but Iris had a hell of a support system from the women in their family. That child was showered with love from all angles, every day of her life. She only hoped Iris wouldn't turn out to be a spoiled little shit because of it.

"Fair enough. But you need to go to college and get a good job so you can help support her. Keep that in mind," Noelle offered.

"You just want me to go to State with you so you don't have to room blind with some weirdo who doesn't shower and wants you to join intermural football."

"I mean, you're not entirely wrong."

Both girls laughed and turned sideways, bumping the metal push bars with their hips to force the side entrance doors open. The wind caught them by surprise as they arrived in the courtyard outside the school.

"Damn, it's Edmund Fitzgerald weather, and it's not even November yet," Noelle said, stopping to zip up her puffy Tommy Hilfiger jacket. "Are you sitting tonight, or do you want to hang?"

"Yeah, the Carter kids and the DeYoung kids. Nancy is going to drop Iris off, too. Apparently, she's going to a concert downstate."

"No fucking way. Did she get Nirvana tickets? She told me she was going to try, but I thought she was full of shit."

Sarah nods. She's wasn't entirely sure how Nancy, a single mother who cleans houses for a living, came up with the money for two concert tickets, gas, and a hotel. Nancy was dodgy when Sarah had asked her about the boy she was going with, so she wondered if he might be involved in some shady business, having that kind of cash.

"Dude, your sister isn't even into grunge. She doesn't deserve to see Kurt Cobain. We do. Well, at least I do."

"Take it up with her, I guess. Anyway, I need to stop by Willow's Nook before she closes for the night; I'll catch up with you tomorrow."

Noelle shook her head but knew better than to say how she really felt. Willow Nora, the owner of Willow's Nook was a certified nutjob. Everyone in Westridge Cove knew she'd lost her mind the day her husband died in 1990. She had spent the entirety of her days trying to magically become a clairvoyant, or a medium, or learn witchcraft, or whatever she thinks will help her communicate with his spirit. She's Looney Tunes. Willow's Nook may advertise itself as a gift shop and bookstore, but the only books she stocks on her shelves would have gotten her burned at the stake three hundred years ago. Sarah carried some sort of fondness for the crazy old bat and spent entirely too much time with her at the store. Noelle had attempted to raise her concerns to Sarah on several occasions, but her words had always fallen on deaf ears.

"Hey, if you have time, you guys can use her special powers to contact JFK and see if he thinks there was a second gunman on the grassy knoll," Noelle shouted as they parted ways a block from the store. "Or maybe you could make me a voodoo doll of Mr. Evans. He gave me detention again, and I'd like to give him a few pokes in the you-know-what."

"Fuck off, Noelle," Sarah hollered back with two middle fingers in the air, catching the crossing guard in her peripheral a little too late. "Sorry, Mrs. Anderson," she muttered in response to the woman's disapproving gaze. Her mom played cribbage with Mrs. Anderson on Wednesday nights, so Sarah could only hope she decided not to rat her out. She'd never hear the end of it if Sheila Thornwick learned her precious daughter was shouting vulgarities in the streets of Westridge Cove, in broad daylight no less.

Downtown Westridge was a ghost town after 5:00 p.m., a fact that Mayor Bradbury had been trying to change for years. He said the town is never going to attract tourists like Marquette (a town of 20,000, which makes it a booming metropolis compared to Westridge Cove) if none of the businesses stay open after dark. Sarah's parents said they don't want the kinds of tourists that come around after dark, anyway. Although the mayor continued to promote new ideas to make Westridge Cove a better place, the attitude of the locals had always been "Change? No, thank you. We'll take our beautiful town exactly as it's always been, and don't be bringing your fancy ideas around here anymore." Despite his desire for Westridge to grow and change, Mayor Bradbury remained a beloved political figure due to his jovial personality and penchant for approving most requests made by the locals, if they donated to his reelection campaign. Beatrice Golden baked her famous apple turnovers for his last mayoral fundraiser and immediately got a stop sign approved for the intersection next to her house. All politicians seemed to have a price tag; Mayor Bradbury's was just very low.

Sarah hurried away from Mrs. Anderson in hopes that she'd be distracted by the crowds of rowdy elementary students approaching and forget all about their little interaction.

Macy, who owned the local coffee shop and deli, exited the front door to retrieve her chalkboard menu from the sidewalk when she spotted Sarah approaching.

"Sarah Thornwick! Is your mother needing chicken salad? I was just about to close up, but I'd be happy to get her a pound before I lock the doors."

Another business closing the minute the high school let out for the day. She kind of saw the mayor's point: They could attract a lot more traffic downtown if the stores stayed open late enough for people to stop by after school or work.

The woman held the front door open with her hip as she set the chalkboard behind her in the restaurant's entryway before flipping the sign on the door around to read CLOSED.

"Not today, Miss Macy. She's got cribbage at the community center, and I think they're making chili. I'm just headed to see Willow," Sarah replied, gesturing down the block to Willow's Nook.

Macy was a peacekeeper and, as Sarah's father liked to

say, "wouldn't say shit if she had a mouthful," but Sarah wasn't stupid. She saw the woman flinch at the mention of Willow's name.

"Well, be careful. There's a storm coming in a few hours, and I'd hate for you to be caught outside in it."

Macy ended the conversation with a curt nod and locked the shop's door behind her, because heaven forbid, she subject herself to another minute of discussing the widow Nora. Even at eighteen years old, Sarah recognized that this town had a penchant for despising what they didn't understand.

Next to Macy's Deli was the hardware store, followed by Quick Eddie's Tax Services, Kirby's Kandies, and Donna's Hair and More. A lifetime of getting her hair trimmed by Angie, and Sarah still couldn't figure out which offerings warranted the "and More" in the title, or why the salon Angie owned was called Donna's, but she supposed there was a good reason for both decisions.

Willow Nora may not be an actual witch, but there must be some sort of magic involved in her operation because Sarah's heartrate always slowed the minute her front door came into view. All her problems seemed to disappear at the mere thought of entering the Nook. She exhaled as she took in the new window display, featuring an incredibly authentic-looking human skull, a framed display of butterfly taxidermy, a Ouija board, and various other trinkets and oddities. Sarah couldn't find the words to explain it, but arriving at Willow's Nook felt like coming home.

Chapter Three

OCTOBER 27TH, 1993

"Okay, girls, we shouldn't be too late. You can call the club if you have any emergencies. We left money on the counter to order pizzas," Carol Carter yelled from the foyer in her sexy devil costume. She didn't receive a response until Maggie stumbled out of the kitchen, furiously rubbing her face with a wet washcloth to remove marker drawings left by the youngest Carter boy. She hadn't been in the house a full three minutes before Jack Carter decided his babysitter needed a ghost tattoo on her forehead, in honor of the upcoming holiday.

"Don't worry about a thing, Mrs. Carter. We'll have them in bed long before you get home. It's going to be a great night—these boys are easy," she said with a wink that didn't quite land because her eye was twitching. Carol Carter reached up to hold her red glittered horns in place as she looked past Maggie and into the living room, which had already descended into chaos. Barrett and Jack were climbing Sarah like a tree, attempting to give her a tattoo that matched her sister's; and the neighbor boys, Logan and Kellen, were each wielding hockey sticks and attempting to take Bridget out at the knees. "Just go," Maggie whispered, clapping her hands together to convince herself in the process. "We've got this."

Carol Carter inhaled deeply and spun to face the door just as her husband honked the horn of his Chevy sedan in the driveway. Maggie watched the woman descend the front steps, plastic pitchfork in hand, and hustle quickly across the sidewalk to the passenger door, shaking her head the entire way. If the Halloween party at the Cove Country Club wasn't her favorite night of the year, she wasn't sure she could have made herself leave the house. They'd only be five miles away; there was no need to worry about the boys. They'd be fine. She had to repeat this to herself several times as her husband backed out of the drive.

Back at the house, Maggie took charge by standing on the coffee table and yelling, "That is enough! Five-minute ceasefire or nobody gets pizza!"

Hockey sticks were dropped, Sarah was released from a headlock, and Bridget crumbled to the floor holding her shins. All three sisters were short of breath from dealing with the out-of-control boys and wondered how they were going to last the night.

"I want anchovies on my pizza," Jack yelled, raising his hand. This caused an eruption of arguments for and against the idea of fish on pizza by all four boys, but none of them were physically assaulting their babysitters, so the girls allowed it. Just as the arguing began to subside, the sound of two taps on the front door quieted everyone. The door swung open and Iris ran full speed inside toward her aunts, with an exhausted looking Nancy lagging behind.

"No girls allowed!" Barrett hollered, thrusting his

hockey stick in the air, but it fell on deaf ears. The other three boys adored Iris, and the Thornwick girls suspected that Barrett did, too. He was simply the oldest, so he had reached the age of pretending to hate anything without a penis, rather than admit he might actually enjoy her company.

"I stopped at Ann's on the way in and I have *Hocus Pocus*," Nancy said, producing the plastic VHS case from behind her back. "But nobody gets to watch it unless you're all nice to each other. That includes Iris. Deal?"

"Deal!" they all shouted in unison, because the thrill of watching a "scary" movie outweighed their desire to terrorize Iris.

Nancy set Iris' *Little Mermaid* backpack on the ground next to the door and waved her sisters over. The kids were now playing with dart guns and not-so-quietly plotting a "kidnapping" of Maggie because she was the smallest of the "adults"—complete with a plan to ask for a ransom of five dollars each. The girls let the half-cocked plans proceed because the kids' conspiratory meeting allowed the sisters a moment of peace.

"So, which one of you little bitches told Mom and Dad that I was going to Kalamazoo?" Nancy asked in a hushed tone that was not nearly hushed enough because the eldest neighbor boy gasped and yelled "Swear jar, Nancy!" from across the room.

"Nobody told them. We're not snitches, Nance," Sarah responded, trying to sound cool in front of her older sister.

Sarah and Nancy both turned toward the two youngest, but neither Bridget nor Maggie responded. They looked at each other and then down at the tile below their feet.

The two eldest sisters gasped.

"It was *both* of you!"

Nancy leaned forward and smacked each of them in the bicep with a closed fist in rapid succession. This made all the children laugh. She motioned for them to go play and give the sisters some space.

"You can't be mad at us, Nance. We're watching your kid for free . . . again," Bridget said with a step away from Nancy, rubbing her arm and preparing for another punch.

"And I'd do the same for any of you. But I'd do it without ratting you out."

"Hey now," Maggie said, stepping between them. At fifteen years old, she was somehow the consistent voice of reason. "In our defense, you never told us *not* to tell Mom and Dad. Where were we supposed to tell them you were? Iris is sleeping over tonight, and if you wanted a made-up back story, you should have given us one."

Nancy didn't have a response to this because, as usual, Maggie was right.

The tension was broken by the shrill ring of the telephone in the kitchen. Maggie jogged over to pick up the receiver from the wall mount.

"Carter residence, this is Margaret Thornwick" she said in a singsong tone. "Yes, yes, sir. We'd be happy to. Okay, thank you, sir. See you soon."

"How many times are you going to say sir? Who was that, the president?" Nancy asked.

"Close. The chief of police. He got called in and he wanted to know if he can drop Walton off."

All three sisters groaned in unison. Walton Parker, the police chief's son, was six-years-old and an absolute menace. The last time the girls watched him, he swallowed his own goldfish and threw a glass plate at Bridget's head. His mother passed away when he was only two, and little Wally made it his mission in life to show his dad how difficult being a single parent could be. Everyone felt for Chief Parker, but nobody volunteered to watch that little nightmare. It was possible to have both sympathy *and* sense.

"What? What was I supposed to say? He obviously knows we're already here babysitting. The Carters or the DeYoungs must have told him we have their boys. It's more money; let's just suck it up. It's only a few hours."

"Well, I'm getting out of here before Rex Parker gets here. The last thing I need is a cop to ruin the vibe before I pregame for this concert," Nancy said, waving Iris over for a goodbye hug.

The girls wondered when their straight-laced older sister became so edgy and rebellious.

"Are you going to tell us who you're going to this concert with? What if you go missing? We won't even know who was in your car," Maggie asked.

"No such luck, snitches," Nancy replied with a wink before bending down to get on Iris' level. "You know I love you, my little flower?"

"I love you, too, mommy," Iris said and scrunched her nose as Nancy planted kisses all over her face.

"And I hope you three feel horrible, because I *am* paying you," Nancy said and produced a crisp twenty-dollar bill for each sister from the bag slung over her shoulder.

"Sixty bucks, Nance? You can't afford this. We were only kidding," Sarah protests, holding the money out in her sister's direction.

"I picked up a few more cleaning gigs. I can afford it; I promise."

She turned to leave before they could argue any further and shut the door behind her as the three remaining sisters were left in stunned silence. They'd been helping with Iris since the day she was born, and Nancy had not once offered to compensate them for their services. Most days, they were lucky to get a *thank you* before she rushed in to pick Iris up in the morning.

"Paying us for babysitting, going to an out-of-town concert," Maggie said. "What is going on with her? Did she win the lottery or something?"

"I don't know, but I'm going to enjoy it while it lasts," Bridget replied, folding the bill and tucking it into her back pocket. One step closer to having wheels.

The three girls couldn't help but be disturbed by their sister doing something so out of character. Although she'd moved out of the house years ago, they still knew her better than anyone. They didn't have much more time to reflect on the situation, as just moments later, Chief Rex Parker rang the doorbell and all but threw his son Wally into the house, followed by a rolled up sleeping bag, before shouting his apologies and returning to his squad car.

It was the equivalent of throwing a bomb into the middle of the room. For the next four hours, the Thornwick sisters didn't have a moment of peace while trying their best to control the six children in their care.

Chapter Four

OCTOBER 27TH, 1993

"Where are we going?" Iris whispered into Maggie's ear as she was carried from her spot on the living room floor.

The sisters had just finished tucking the Carter boys into their beds and the two DeYoung boys and Wally Parker into their sleeping bags on the floor of the boys' room.

"Sweetie, you're just going into the guest room to sleep for a few hours until the boys' parents come home. Then I'll wake you up and you can come home with us for a sleepover at Grandma and Grandpa's house," Maggie whispered back.

"But, I don't want to sleep all alone in there," Iris pleaded, rubbing her eyes. "The goblins and the witches will get me."

"I'll leave the door open so you can come see us any time you're scared. We will be right down the hall in the living room. If you're a good girl and get some sleep, I promise we'll make Mickey Mouse pancakes in the morning. I bet we can even convince Grandma to add extra whipped cream. Deal?"

This seemed to pacify Iris, who nodded and rested her head back on Maggie's shoulder, her tiny arms wrapped around her aunt's neck.

The sisters hadn't seen *Hocus Pocus* when it was in theaters that summer and were surprised by a few of the scenes; they were a little frightening for the movie's PG rating. Iris was terrified by the flying witches, and the boys tried to play it cool, but when Billy Butcherson came back to life, she saw at least two of them cover their eyes. The girls were speechless when the boys asked why a virgin had to light the candle, followed by asking what a virgin even was. It took nearly an hour to calm everyone down and get them ready for bed. The rolling thunder outside didn't help their cause. Those kids came up with every excuse in the book as to why they should be allowed to stay up a little later, but the sisters were spent. Sarah finally put her foot down and told them that if they didn't cooperate, she'd use her direct line to Santa and let him know exactly how bad they'd been tonight. They were lights out within fifteen minutes.

Maggie returned to the living room, sans Iris, and collapsed onto her back on the thick, plush turquoise carpet.

"That was a lot of work," mumbled Bridget, horizontal on one of the couches.

"We're going to have to start putting a limit on the number of boys we'll watch at one time. The girls are fine, but the boys? I can't do it anymore," Sarah added. "They are monsters."

"If they were all like Iris, we could watch twenty kids at once. I don't know how Nancy did it, but she raised the most well-behaved kid in town," Maggie said. "Don't let me forget—I promised her Mickey Mouse pancakes in the morning before we go to school."

"I've got to get up early to study for chem anyway; I'll make them," Bridget offered.

"Don't forget the whipped cream. Last time she was pretty torn up about it," Sarah reminded her.

All three girls shot straight up to a sitting position when the front door of the house swung open without warning. Maybe the movie had them a little on edge, as well—not that they'd ever admit it.

Nancy slipped inside the house with red-rimmed eyes and puffy cheeks. She was wearing a tightly fitting black mini dress and heels—not the typical outfit for a grunge concert. She was obviously fighting to keep it together but broke down sobbing when she saw her sisters. They each leapt to their feet and rushed to her.

"Nance, what the hell happened? Are you okay?" Sarah asked, visibly searching her for injuries. "Did you get in an accident?"

"No, no," she said before losing her composure once more.

"Hey, hey, it's okay Nance. Just take a deep breath. Come sit in the living room and tell us what happened," Maggie offered, steering her sister to the couch closest to the door.

"It . . . It just didn't work out. It wasn't a good idea," Nancy said, her eyes unable to meet her sisters'.

"What didn't work out? The concert? The guy? I knew it was a guy," Bridget said, snapping her fingers. "I fucking knew it."

"None of it. I just really don't want to talk about it, guys. I'm just so tired. I want to get Iris and go home and sleep for twelve hours."

They looked at each other over the top of Nancy's downturned head and silently debated if they were going to let it go or press for more information. With a shrug, Sarah decided that they should just let it go, at least for now. They could get it out of her once she'd had some sleep.

"Well, you can't sleep that long because we promised Iris her favorite pancakes before she goes to school. Are you sure you don't want us to just take her home so you can rest?" Maggie offered.

Nancy raised her head and managed a slight smile. "I'm sure, Mags. I don't want to go to bed without her. I shouldn't have even planned to be away tonight. She deserves to wake up with me there."

"Well, let us give you the money back," Maggie declared, standing to retrieve the twenty from her pocket.

"No, no. Consider it a downpayment for the debt I owe you girls for always watching her," Nancy replied, waving her away.

None of the girls argued because not only was she right, but they were all trying to save money for their own goals that year. Sarah for life after high school, Bridget for a car, and Maggie for a new wardrobe to keep up with the popular girls at school.

"She's in the guest bedroom down the hall. I'll get her bag for you," Maggie offered.

Nancy went to retrieve her daughter and returned with a small sack of dead weight, wrapped in a pink blanket and thrown over her right shoulder.

"Was she good?" Nancy whispered.

"She always is," Maggie said with a wink, placing Iris' small backpack over her sister's shoulder.

"I appreciate you guys. I hope you know that," Nancy

told them, wrapping her hand around Iris' head so it didn't hit the door frame on her way out.

Nancy gave one last wave as she closed the door behind her, leaving her sisters to finish their babysitting shift.

She'll play this scene over and over in her mind, trying to remember every detail she can because as they stand in that living room waving goodbye, it's the last time she'd ever see her sisters again.

Chapter Five

"Did you hear what happened in Burntwood?" Nancy asks, wiping the counter with a spray bottle of homemade cleaner she swears by, but she also refuses to give anyone the recipe.

"You're going to have to be more specific, Mom," I say, doing my best to keep my facial expressions in check. I know exactly what happened in Burntwood. Obviously.

"A young man's body was found at the bottom of the cliffs, and he had a note in his pocket, confessing to being the *Burntwood Burglar*. After all this time, it was some college kid who moved up here from Chicago. Could have knocked me over with a feather when I heard the news."

Some college kid was an asshole named Chad who terrorized local women who lived alone, following them home from the bars and assaulting them before taking anything of value from their homes. Luckily, that *kid from Chicago* got a rude awakening two nights ago when Lucy and I taught him a very important lesson about accountability. Soon, the crime lab will match his DNA to that left at the seven crime scenes, and the case will be closed. He was wracked with guilt, so he wrote a confession letter and threw himself from the cliffs. A tragedy, really.

"Better close the border to the U.P. and quit letting those bastards from Illinois in, eh?" I ask.

Lucy spits out her coffee from a booth behind me, quickly wiping her mouth and pretending she simply choked on it, so my mom won't lecture her on decency. Nothing really scares Lucy like Nancy Thornwick does.

"This is not a joke, Iris. Tomorrow is October first. The tourists have already started arriving. Hank and Cora said they're at full capacity until mid-November at the inn. Another tragedy is not what we need right now."

I have the barstools flipped upside down, tightening their screws before the lunch rush. Do the screws need to be tightened? Probably not. Does my mom have it on the schedule for the last day of the month, every month? She sure does. The tightest screwed barstools in Westridge Cove —you'll find them at the Thornwick Café. We could add it to the sign, right under SOUPS, SALADS, SANDWICHES, AND GOOD TIMES.

"A serial predator being found at the bottom of the cliffs isn't what I'd call a tragedy. Maybe the women of Burntwood will sleep a little easier tonight. Plus, every tourist coming to Westridge Cove is here for action. The macabre, the spooky, the unexplained; that's why they make the trip. A man throwing himself to his death is just what they want to hear about when they arrive in town. It'll be fine, Mom. Death is good for business, remember?"

I turn back to Lucy, who shrugs. She's stacking creamer cups into a makeshift castle. Heaven forbid she help me tighten these damn barstools or assist with anything else around the café. "I'm not technically an employee anymore; it sounds like a liability issue," she likes to remind me when I give her the death stare. "I'd hate for there to be a lawsuit tainting our friendship."

Lucy quit working at Thornwick Café a little over a year ago, which was for the best. Take my advice: If you spend every waking moment with your best friend, please don't also work with them. It's a recipe for pointless arguing. We get along much better now that we're not working side by side for forty hours a week before clocking out and spending even more time together.

"Did I tell you one of those big news outlets is coming to town tomorrow?" Mom asks me. "They're doing a segment called, 'Westridge Cove: Salem of the Midwest' and want to interview people around town about how tourism has affected our livelihoods." She's wiping furiously at a spot on the counter that's already been clean for twenty minutes. Mom is wound tightly today, but this happens every fall. I try to prepare her each August for the inevitable, but she says the same thing every year: *Iris, it's been decades. I'm fine. It's just a season like any other. In fact, it's the best season because it gets us caught up on bills.*

"Want me to give them a sound bite? Hi, I'm Iris Thornwick, which means this infamous tragedy has been horrible for our family, but fabulous for business. Now stop on down to Thornwick Café, where you can have two-for-one cinnamon rolls the size of your head while you stare at us Thornwicks and wonder if we're witches, too!" I wiggle my fingers for added effect.

I can feel Lucy holding her breath behind me when Mom shouts, "Iris Elizabeth Thornwick! That is not even close to being funny. We are not profiting off my sisters; we just happen to have a café that bears our last name in a town that seems obsessed with what happened to them."

My eyes travel up to the hanging witch décor, dangling from every light fixture in our restaurant. Outside the door, there's a seven-foot sign welcoming tourists to Westridge Cove, home of the infamous missing Thornwick sisters. The stack of flyers next to the cash register, listing all of the October festivities scheduled in town for the anniversary of their disappearance.

"Okay, Mom," I say, tight-lipped. I'm in no mood for an argument today.

That's the part nobody talks about when a tragedy of this magnitude strikes: Your name no longer belongs to you. Your family's name becomes public property, and in our case, it's worn on the T-shirts and hats of half the tourists who arrive in Westridge Cove every fall.

Sarah.

Bridget.

Margaret.

The Thornwick Sisters.

Until October of 1993, very few people outside of the Upper Peninsula had heard their names. They lived normal, small-town teenage lives with breaking curfew and failing algebra among their worst offenses. Our family was well respected in the community and had escaped the normal scandals that plagued families in our area—drug addiction, crime, alcoholism, adultery. The only red mark in an otherwise unblemished file would be my mother getting pregnant with me at eighteen, father unknown.

The night those three sisters agreed to babysit a group of unruly elementary school kids, myself included, would change the course of history in this sleepy little town.

Chapter Six

OCTOBER 27TH, 1993

Before the sisters had a free moment to discuss Nancy's odd behavior, there was another knock at the door of the Carter household.

Maggie, who always seemed to be the one to hop up and answer the phone or the door, even at their own house, jogged over to the entryway in her lace-trimmed ankle socks, quick to answer before another knock could wake the children.

"What's up, sluts?"

It was Ann Haven, Sarah's friend and daughter of Mr. and Mrs. Haven, owners of Westridge Rentals. Procurer of the *Hocus Pocus* advance copy and regular supplier of campy horror VHS tapes that the teenage girls had no business watching. Like clockwork, she whipped out a hand from behind her back and was clutching a copy of *Candyman.*

"I can't watch that again. Last time I couldn't look in my

mirror for days. I kept seeing that damn bloody hook jumping out at me," Bridget said, shaking her head.

"I've never seen it," Maggie added, taking the plastic case from Ann's hand and inspecting the back cover. "Killer bees? An urban legend? I'm in."

"Mags, you'll be scared out of your mind," Bridget told her.

Sarah stood from the couch, ejected the *Hocus Pocus* tape from the VCR, and placed it back in its case. As she was walking by Bridget to grab the copy of *Candyman*, she said, "She's fifteen years old. We were watching scary movies with Ann a whole lot younger than that. If she wants to watch it, let's watch it."

Bridget shrugged and rolled her eyes. She was sick of Sarah naming herself the ringleader, that designation based solely on birth order. She had her shit together better than Sarah any day of the week, yet Sarah got to call the shots because Bridget dared to be born two years after she came into the world. She never pulled rank on Maggie because she knew how much it sucked, and wouldn't dare put her through it. As far as she could tell, Nancy didn't do it to Sarah, either. She was too busy trying to hold down a job and raise Iris. The only victims of the birth-order hierarchy seemed to be the ones directly below Sarah.

The argument was resolved with Bridget once again getting the short end of the stick, so they all settled in to watch a movie that had haunted her nightmares since the day she first watched it months prior. Of course it was cool that Ann could get free rentals any time she wanted from her parents' store, but would it kill her to get a feel-good flick once in a while? One that didn't involve someone's internal organs being infested by bees—that would be a welcome change.

Exactly one hour and thirty-nine minutes later, they all regretted their decision to watch the movie. The Carter house was over sixty years old and had chosen that very moment to start serenading them with knocking pipes and creaky floorboards, despite nobody walking on them. The wind outside had kicked up a few notches, and all four girls startled when a large tree branch slapped the side of the house after a particularly strong gust.

"We should turn some lights on," said Bridget, scrambling to her feet and pretending to be unbothered by the litany of unexplainable sounds.

"Come on, where's the fun in that?" Ann asked.

"What do you mean? The movie is over, time to turn the lights back on," Maggie told her, wishing she'd sided with Bridget from the start.

"Well, we have to try it," Sarah chimed in. "Let's just go to the bathroom down the hall. We'll say his name five times and if nothing happens, we can turn all the lights back on. Deal?"

Despite a few words of protest, several eye rolls, and crossed arms, eventually they gave in. All four girls traveled down the hallway like they were walking to their death. By the time they got to the bathroom, which was even darker than the rest of the house, nobody wanted to go through with it, but none of them wanted to be the one to chicken out.

"Okay, who is going to say it? Does it have to be the same person?" Ann asked.

"Let's just get it over with," Maggie said, quickly adding, "Candyman, Candyman, Candyman, Candyman, Candy—"

"Wait," Bridget interrupted her. "Be sure before you say it a fifth time." She quickly grew angry at her hands for betraying her body. They were shaking as she held them up toward her younger sister.

"Candyman," Sarah finished, and before the word was completely out of her red, popsicle-stained lips, the shower curtain behind them blew forward, and a thud echoed in the dark, quiet room. All four of them screamed so loud, they probably woke up the entire neighborhood.

"Blackjack!" Maggie yelled, pointing at the Carter's black cat, who had just jumped out of his favorite sleeping spot, the bathtub. "You scared the shit out of us!"

Sarah held a finger to her lips, motioning for the girls to stay quiet so they could listen for tiny footsteps above them. Surely, those screams woke the kids up, and they would be back to square one regarding getting them back to bed.

They stood like that for minutes—motionless, but each with a heart beating so loudly they swore the other three must have been able to hear it.

Nothing. Not a creak of the floorboard, not a whimper, just total silence. Those boys must have been sleeping like the dead to not be awakened by the commotion.

"Let's do *Bloody Mary* now," Maggie said, clapping her hands together. This got a great laugh out of the group because now the youngest of the bunch was the one with all the courage to proceed with the urban legends. "I'm not scared anymore. This is fun."

Once they'd completed a few rounds of *Bloody Mary* in the mirror, no jumping cats to disrupt the show this time, they moved back to the living room and played any game they could possibly think of that might feel spooky. They were riddled with fear each time a gust of wind caused the trees to create a symphony of cracks and whistles, and then they'd erupt in fits of laughter each time they reasoned with themselves about the sounds.

Sitting cross-legged in a circle, the girls lit three half-used Shopko candles they found in Mrs. Carter's junk drawer with a lighter that Ann had in the pocket of her jean jacket. Sarah drew a makeshift Ouija board from memory on a blank piece of paper, and they used a flat letter opener bearing the logo of the local credit union as their planchette. It didn't have a small window like a true planchette, so they decided that whichever letter the end of the blade was pointing to shall officially be the letter the spirit had chosen. They explained it out loud to any ghosts that may be in the room with them, so they'd know the rules.

"Whichever spirits may be present in this home, please respond to our questions by moving this letter opener. None of us are going to be moving it on our own," Ann explained out loud, shooting a look of warning at each of the girls. "So, when it moves to a certain word or letter, we will know it's you doing it."

None of the girls really knew anybody who had died, so they made the obvious choice to try and contact the spirit of Elvis Presley.

"Did you really eat peanut butter and banana sandwiches?" Bridget asked, focused on the paper before her. Each girl had her pointer and middle finger on the letter opener, with Sarah quite obviously the ringleader, pushing the indicator toward YES. With each movement, the letter-sized sheet of printer paper crinkled over the carpet it was laid on.

"Hold on, I'm going to grab a piece of cardboard from the garage to set this on so we can have a steady surface," Maggie said.

"Or we could just play something else," Ann suggested. The girls were torn between agreeing and simply passing out in their respective spots on the floor. They were all exhausted, and it was a school night, after all. Surely the Carters, DeYoungs, and Chief Parker would be back soon.

"We could play *Light as a Feather, Stiff as a Board*," Sarah suggested. "I haven't played it since eighth grade at Marsha Reilly's house."

"Three people aren't enough to lift anyone with our fingers, even if it works. We'd need more to play," Bridget pointed out.

As if being summoned, Logan Carter padded out of his room in his *Ghostbusters* pajamas and called out to the girls from upstairs.

"Where's my mom and dad?" he asked, rubbing his eyes.

"Yeah, why are you guys still here?" added Kellen DeYoung, who was now beside him.

The girls glanced upstairs to see all five boys leaning against the spindles on the railing outside their room. They weren't sure how long the kids had been watching them play sleepover games.

Before the girls could answer, the entire pack made their way down the stairs. The winds outside had kicked up another notch, and the continuing sounds of thunder boomed in the distance.

"What are you guys playing?" Wally Parker asked. Being half asleep is the only time this kid would be calm enough to form a complete sentence without bouncing around the room before he could finish.

Ann raised her eyebrows at the girls a few times and winked.

"We're about to play a game called *Light as a Feather, Stiff as a Board,* and it's really fun. Do you guys want to play?"

Chapter Seven

PRESENT DAY

"Wally Fucking Parker," I mutter under my breath so the two old-timers sitting at the counter don't hear me.

Lucy is still here, at the far end of the bar, doodling witches on a placemat. She's avoiding something; I just haven't yet figured out what it is. She's been at the café for hours.

"Say what you want about him, but he's grown up to be fine as hell, and you know it. Maybe you should drop the lifelong vendetta against him, and your ridiculous vow of chastity. Give the man a chance," she tells me.

"I don't have a vow of chastity," I respond, squinting my eyes. I've walked to the end of the bar because, like most of our conversations, nobody else needs to hear this.

"You sure as fuck act like you do," she quips, sipping her tea and looking out the window that faces the parking lot. "Here he comes now; get that shit out of your teeth and act like a lady."

Without thinking, my right hand flies up to my mouth before I see her wicked grin. She's messing with me.

"Seems like you *do* care what ol' Wally thinks, my friend."

"I do not," I whisper. "Wally Parker is a pain in my ass," I say a little louder this time. I'm not sure if it's for my own benefit.

"You could do worse than Chief Parker," one of the men at the bar tells me as I approach him to refill his mug of house coffee. "We'd all like to see you find a husband, sweetheart."

It's been nearly thirty-three years since Wally's dad made the last-minute decision to drop him off at the Carter house to be babysat the night my aunts went missing. These days, Rex is in an assisted living home, and Wally has moved up the ranks of Westridge Cove Public Safety. He now has the position his dad held for over three decades, chief of police. If you think that title holds any weight in my eyes, you'd be wrong. Wally has been a thorn in my side since we were kids, and a badge and fancy title aren't going to change that. Sometimes I come to a rolling stop at the four-way in front of Northwood Grocery and dare him to pull me over with a wink. He always sits in that cruiser shaking his head at me, but I consider that to be a victory in our little game of chicken. He likes to remind me that in bigger jurisdictions, the chief of police is far too busy to be working traffic stops and that I'm lucky he doesn't haul me in for wasting his precious time. I'd like to see him try.

"Afternoon, Iris," Wally says, walking through the front door.

I wrinkle my nose and roll my eyes. It's the best I can do on short notice. Normally, I'd have a witty comeback to his greeting, but I've spent the last forty-five seconds convincing my best friend and two of my regulars that I don't have feelings for this man. It knocked me off my game.

"Chief Parker, is it true they found the body of that little pervert over in Burntwood?" one of the men asks as Wally sits down to their right and directly in front of me. I get a whiff of his cologne, which I guess smells nice. I set down a menu and placemat, like he doesn't order the same thing every time he comes in. I like to keep him humble.

"Now, Gerry, you know that's not my jurisdiction, so I don't suppose I have any statement to make on the matter."

Both men look at Wally, knowing damn well he'll give them *something*. He can't just leave them high and dry. They both have bowling league tonight at the Elks Lodge, and it would give them great pleasure to stroll in with insider information before they knock down their first pins.

"Let's just say, off the record, that your daughters and granddaughters can sleep well tonight. There is no longer a threat of the Burntwood Burglar striking again," Wally says with a wink.

I once again roll my eyes. Heaven forbid the truth ever get in the way of his heroics. Chief Wally Parker had nothing to do with the capture and/or death of the Burntwood Burglar. Not that he'll ever know it, but the credit goes to Lucy and me. We are the reason the women of Burntwood and beyond won't need to look over their shoulders when they walk home tonight. The unsung heroes of Gallows County.

After a few "atta boys" and pats on the back, Wally turns to me expectantly. "I'll just have the usual, Iris." This man is wearing a smile like he just scored the winning touchdown at the state championship game. He was asleep in his bed, probably dreaming of issuing speeding tickets to single mothers, while Lucy and I were doing his job for him.

"Sorry, Chief Parker, you haven't been in all week, and I can't seem to remember what you usually order."

He smirks.

He hasn't changed his order in years.

The men next to him even know what he orders, and their shoulders bounce with silent chuckles at my little game.

"Did Wally ever tell you guys about how he taught me to shoot? That's right; over at the Gallows County Range. By the third day, my aim was so true, he got his feelings hurt and quit offering to give me lessons. I guess the student surpassed the teacher a little quicker than he'd hoped," I tell the guys.

Wally gives me a look as if to say, *Oh, are we bringing up old stories now?*

"Did you gentlemen know that Iris and I went to the Homecoming dance together sophomore year? I drove her all the way to the Stonehouse in Delta County because she said it was her favorite. She ordered the most expensive thing on the menu, and I barely had enough gas money left to get back to Westridge. After all that, she had the nerve to dance with Bradley Lamarche, right in front of me."

Both men raise their eyebrows in anticipation of more details regarding our one night of teenage romance.

"Did you gentlemen also know that I punched Wally so hard after the little league championship game in 1999 that I broke his nose? If you look at it closely, you can still see that the bridge is a little crooked," I counter. "I clocked him good, and he knows I could do it again."

They lean in close to Wally to get a better look when he holds a hand up over his precious nose to stop the inspection.

"Okay, that's enough of this trip down memory lane.

Could I please get a black coffee and a club sandwich on rye so I can eat and be on my way?"

Now he won't even make eye contact with me, which means I win.

"Would you like that rye bread toasted, Wally?"

He rubs the bridge of his nose, as if the bruising has reappeared after twenty-seven years.

"You know damn well I like it toasted, Iris."

Chapter Eight

PRESENT DAY

I'm leaning my elbows on the bar and watching the local news as I wait for the night crew to come in for shift change. I traded a few more barbs back and forth with ol' Wally, much to the pleasure of Lucy and the two regulars, and then he cashed out and left me the usual twenty percent tip before retreating with his tail between his legs, because I remain sharper and funnier than he'll ever be.

Bucky and Brighton Lancaster, Westridge Cove's version of the Rockefellers, are on the screen being interviewed by one of our local anchors. Nobody has capitalized on my aunts' disappearances more than the damn Lancasters.

Plenty of out-of-towners showed up for the search parties in the days following the news that three sisters had vanished into thin air. Various television stations came to Westridge to cover the case. It received national attention for a few months before a bigger story took over the headlines. All three sisters were legally declared dead in 2000, and that's when the general public decided it was fair game to celebrate their deaths every year like it was fucking Mardi Gras.

Since the day Westridge Cove became "Salem of the Midwest," or "The Great Lakes Own Witch City," the Lancasters have opened the Thornwick Witch Museum, the Westridge Cove Theatre (with productions featuring reenactments of my aunts' final days, running each fall), the Haunted Hotel (they ran out of steam naming that one, eh?), and numerous gift shops scattered throughout the town. They also own several properties leased out by local businesses, all under the umbrella of Lancaster Enterprises. I'm sure you can imagine how I feel about local power couple Bucky and Brighton Lancaster.

"Mr. Lancaster, what does Westridge Cove have in store for tourists this October?" the interviewer asks. They are standing in front of the museum, located on the busiest corner in town.

"I'm glad you asked, Sophia," he says, with a discreet wink he saves only for every attractive female on the planet. "If you go to Westridge Cove's website, you'll find a list of exciting events for this year's attendees. From the parade tomorrow that kicks off the month of October, to the carnival in Cameron Park, Kayla's famous haunted corn maze, and the guided nightly tours, we have something for everyone. We are thrilled that this event has grown yearly, and this year we are expecting the biggest crowds yet. If you want to commemorate your annual visit to Westridge Cove, our gift shops have four locations throughout the town for all your souvenir needs."

Oh, did I mention that Bucky Lancaster is also the mayor of Westridge Cove now? Yep, he ran unopposed in

2002 and has been reelected without an opponent ever since. Our former mayor, Bill Bradbury, resigned when Lancaster announced his candidacy and now lives in a beautiful lakefront home in Traverse City. According to social media, he also takes two to three beach vacations every year and drives a brand-new Lexus SUV. This is all on a schoolteacher's pension, which was his day job while he was our beloved mayor. A mayor who would have been reelected easily, regardless of the opponent. Suddenly, he's gone and Bucky Lancaster gets elected again every term, without effort. I don't mean to be a conspiracy theorist, but as the saying goes, "Follow the money."

"Iris, you need to learn to wipe that scowl off your face whenever you see Bucky Lancaster. The last thing we need is a rumor starting that we don't support the mayor," Mom says, setting down a rack of clean silverware in front of me to roll.

"Why would we not support a millionaire grifter who profits off the deaths of your sisters? That'd be insane, right? What will the townsfolk say? I'll be sure to smile every time I see him promoting T-shirts with their faces on them from now on, Mom. I sure am sorry."

She puts both hands on the counter to brace herself and exhales as if she cannot fathom a person more difficult than me, her only daughter, who insists on bringing truth to every conversation.

"Iris, please," she says, looking defeated. "He's a big reason why we are able to pay our mortgage. He's helped grow tourism in Westridge to a level we never thought possible."

"Mom, you sound like a spokesperson for his office. You can't honestly continue to support this man? The only reason this town has a tourism industry is because your sisters are dead. And every time someone else dies in this town, the lore grows and the dollar bills stack up. Death. That's what he's used to grow business, Mom."

"He's not as bad as you think, Iris. Just because he has money doesn't make him the enemy."

It's all I can do not to laugh hysterically. My mom used to clean their house—well, one of their houses; I believe they have two vacation homes as well—and she has defended him ever since. I'll never understand. Part of me thinks her reaction is not so much in defense of Bucky, but rather a strange desire to keep the peace in every situation, no matter how many assholes may be involved. My mother cannot stand criticism, fighting, or even healthy debate. I'm not sure if it's a defense mechanism since her sisters disappeared or something she learned in therapy, but she'd like the entire town to hold hands and sing while rainbows shoot out of our assholes, three hundred sixty-five days a year. And she's not even medicated; it's just how her brain is wired.

"Anyway, when Nikki gets here to relieve you, could you please drop off this soup at Willow's on your way home? She said she's had a sore throat and a case of the sneezes, so maybe just ring her bell and leave it at the door."

"Not a case of the sneezes," I respond, but quickly recover when I sense that she's at her limit with my sarcasm. "Yes, Mom. I'd be happy to."

Although I'm not as close to Willow Nora as my aunt Sarah was, I do understand why she was so drawn to the woman. Sure, she's a little kooky, but she's also the most interesting person I've ever met. I don't tend to buy into the whole idea of black magic and the world of witchcraft, but I must admit that some of her "spells" and "remedies" have brought me dangerously close to being a believer. She even added the word *apothecary* to her business name, which is now Willow's Nook and Apothecary, because so many people have been helped by her little remedies.

I'm surprised she even has a cold; normally she'd brew some concoction of sage ginseng flower and boo-boo root or whatever and *boom*, she'd be healed. One time when I was a kid, I fell off my bike and skinned my knees so badly, it hurt to wear pants. She rubbed some sort of oil on it, and they were healed by the next day. My mother made me promise not to tell my grandparents that she let Willow treat me. It was "our little secret."

My mom has made it her mission to look after Willow in the years since my aunts disappeared. In a town this small and close-minded, they don't take kindly to people they view as "different." They sure as hell don't accept someone like Willow Nora, who regularly dabbles in the unexplained, owns an oddities shop, and was one of the last people known to see my aunts alive.

Chapter Nine

OCTOBER 28TH, 1993

I f it were possible for an alarm clock to inflict physical pain, all three Thornwick sisters would have been victims that morning. They were at the Carters' house until nearly one o'clock in the morning before they were relieved of their duties for the night.

Sure, they received a few extra bucks for staying late, but they didn't get home and in bed until two, which meant they were all operating on about four hours of sleep.

"I'm not sure you girls should be taking babysitting gigs on weeknights anymore. I can't stand to see you like this. Maggie, you're fifteen years old—you shouldn't know what it's like to have bags under your eyes yet," their mother told them as she dished out bacon and eggs onto each of their plates. Thursday morning was bacon and eggs day, regardless of how tired they were. Sheila Thornwick was nothing if not a keeper of family traditions.

"We need the money, Mom," Bridget told her, forking her eggs on top of the bacon and back onto the plate again.

"You live at home and don't have any bills. Also, quit playing with your food. You girls need a good breakfast so you can have the energy to focus while you're at school today. Nobody has any extracurriculars tonight, so you can all take nice naps before supper time."

"You know I'm saving up for a car," Bridget reminded her. "Every dollar counts."

Sheila cocked her head and gazed at her sixteen-year-old. She didn't know where the time had gone. Just yesterday, she was learning to ride a bike without training wheels. Within four years, Sheila and Peter wouldn't have any children at home. She couldn't bear the thought of an empty nest. Who would she make breakfast for? What would she do with all the time she'd spent washing the girls' laundry for the last two decades? She might consider getting a part-time job, just to keep her mind on something other than missing her girls.

"Well, did you girls at least have a good time? Were the boys well-behaved?"

"Yeah, Chief Parker ended up dropping off Wally because he got called into work. He was a pain in the ass, but not nearly as bad as last time. Maybe because the Carters didn't have a goldfish he could swallow," Sarah deadpanned as she squirted ketchup on top of her eggs, causing Maggie to wrinkle her nose.

"I expected Iris to be here when we woke up. I'm assuming Nancy ended up driving back from the concert early?" Sheila asked.

"Oh, we forgot to tell you: There's a bunch of drama there. She didn't go to the concert, and she showed up to pick up Iris and was super upset. She sure as hell wasn't dressed like she planned to go to see Nirvana, but she wouldn't tell us what happened," Bridget said, not taking her eyes off her plate.

Sitting on the middle barstool at the breakfast counter, she's slapped in unison by both sisters. Nancy had just chewed their heads off for being snitches, and here she was, spilling the beans to their mother. Bridget rubbed both arms where she was hit and shrugged.

"That was unnecessary. She obviously sees that Iris isn't here. She deserves to know."

"Mom, just do us a solid and let Nancy tell you what happened. She's been on our case about telling you guys her business, and we just want to keep the peace. I'm sure you understand," Sarah said, playing to her mother's soft spot of keeping the peace.

Reluctantly, Sheila nodded. Just yesterday she was changing their diapers, and now they're banding together to keep secrets from her.

"Okay, I won't tell her that you girls said anything. But if she's struggling, I need to know about it. I'm her mother. And Iris doesn't need to be around a Sad Sack Sally of a mother; I'll tell you that much. I was just reading an article about how your general temperament can rub off on your children in ways you'd never imagine. *Reader's Digest* had a whole write up about it. I'll do some investigating when I see her this weekend and see what I can come up with."

All three girls know their mother well enough to know that "do some investigating" translates to she's going to show up at Nancy's apartment and perform the worst acting job of her life while saying she was just in the neighborhood and thought she'd drop in. Within minutes, Nancy will know that her sisters ratted her out, and she'll most likely be at the house waiting to inflict pain on them when they get home from school. Typical older sister behavior.

"Okay, we've got to get to school," Maggie said, ever the responsible one of the group. "Bridget, don't forget your science project."

"Shit," Bridget said, remembering the plant-growth experiment she left scattered across one of their dad's work benches in the garage.

"Language," Sheila told her, grabbing each of their plates to stack in the sink. "I packed it up for you last night to make it easier to take to school. It's right outside the back door."

Bridget exhaled; once again, her mom saved the day. That was Sheila Thornwick's superpower—making everyone else's lives easier. The girls were too young to notice that nobody was working to do the same for Sheila.

"Thank you, Mom. Will you tell Dad we love him when he gets up and that we hope he has a good day at work?" Bridget asked.

When they got home in the middle of the night from babysitting, their dad still had a few hours left on his shift at the mill. They didn't know how he could stay awake all night during these shutdown shifts, let alone operate heavy equipment. Maggie was talking about it at school with her lab partner, Jessa, when she asked what shutdown meant.

"You know . . . I'm not really sure. I just know it's a lot of hours and he's like a zombie when he's not at work during those weeks."

Jessa gave her a flash of judgement but reeled it in when she realized she didn't actually know what her father did at the insurance agency, either. Leave for work in a suit, come home from work in a suit that is slightly wrinkled, and pay for the household expenses so her mother could stay at home. That's what he did. The details of their fathers' jobs were not for teenagers to concern themselves with.

Sarah, Bridget, and Maggie did all they could to stay awake through the final bell that day. Sarah's moment of weakness came during fifth hour when Mrs. Davis put on an American Revolution documentary, and the sound of cannons somehow soothed her into a slumber, right there at her desk. It's not something that she was proud of, but she had to flirt with Dennis O'Conner to give her the answers to the pop quiz after the film. He suggested they go to the mall together after school, to which she handed his answers back and replied, "Maybe some other time, Denny."

None of the girls had the energy to socialize with their friends on the way home that day. Sarah didn't stop at Willow's Nook, Maggie didn't wait for Jessa to catch up with her, and Bridget didn't have it in her to ride her bike; she just held the handlebars and walked it home.

Their paths converged about two blocks from home, and the three sisters wordlessly made the rest of the trek home together. Once their house came into sight, they noticed a strange car in the driveway.

"Is that Mrs. DeYoung's car?" Maggie asked, referring to the mother of the neighbor boys they babysat the night before.

"I think so, but she doesn't usually hang out with Mom. That's strange," Bridget replied. "Maybe she's selling her Avon or something."

As they neared the house, Karen DeYoung was exiting through the front door. She looked at the girls like they had three heads before pulling her purse closer to her body. She made direct eye contact with all three before hurrying to her car and shutting the door. Within seconds, the girls heard the automatic locks popping shut.

"What in the world?" Sarah whispered.

The night before, when the parents came to relieve the

girls, Mrs. DeYoung was slightly inebriated but incredibly kind and thankful to the sisters for watching Logan and Kellen so she and her husband could enjoy the Halloween party. She arrived within minutes of Chief Parker, who shared in her gratitude. Sarah remembered thinking that it was worth the late night because it felt so good to help these parents enjoy themselves. She even tipped the girls an extra twenty-dollar bill to split. Now she was looking at them like they wore scarlet letters on their chests.

Without a word, Karen backed out of the Thornwick driveway, put the car in drive, and pressed on the gas a little too hard on her way out, causing gravel to kick up behind her sedan.

The sisters shared a look and a shrug before walking around the house to enter through the kitchen.

When they did, they found their mother sitting at the dining room table. There were two empty coffee mugs in front of her, a red lipstick stain on Karen's, and her fingers were weaved through her hair at the scalp. With inflamed eyes and a pile of used tissue on the table in front of her, Sheila Thornwick raised her head to meet the gaze of her three youngest daughters.

"Girls, sit down. We need to talk about last night."

Chapter Ten

PRESENT DAY

Every year we have a meeting at town hall on the last day of September, and every year it erupts into chaos for the following reasons:

1. Mayor Lancaster (a.k.a. Butthole Bucky, as Lucy and I have been calling him for years) announces a big change in that year's festivities, and the townspeople revolt because one day is clearly not enough time to accommodate his request. Bucky reminds them that changing our mindset is what has made this town profitable, and we need to trust his judgement. Change is good. This is usually when I roll my eyes, and my mom discreetly kicks my foot from the chair next to me.

2. Steve, the owner of the art gallery in town, stands up and declares that he doesn't care about the money. It's against his artistic

integrity to cater to tourists, rather than those who love and appreciate art. He is reminded by several of his neighbors and friends, as well as the mayor, that if it were not for this month-long tourist season, he wouldn't be able to pay rent year-round on that gallery. He sits down in a fit of defeat and exhales loudly while shaking his head. This performance is so that he can retain his credibility as an artist, but deep down, Steve Garbugli can't wait to jack up his prices and swipe those out-of-state credit cards for thirty-one days straight.

3. Sweet, sweet Hank and Cora Herbert, who own the Westridge Inn Bed and Breakfast, attempt to make this whole ordeal easier on my mother and me. They remind their fellow business owners that this financial windfall is fantastic for all of us, but let us not forget that it is due to the horrible disappearances and presumed deaths of three teenagers. They suggest that all businesses donate a portion of their sales in October directly to our family, or to a scholarship in my aunts' names, or to some other foundation they think would soften the blow of our family tragedy becoming a yearly festival. Each year, they propose these ideas, and each year we stand and refuse. It's become a symbolic routine, really.

People wonder how we can stay in this town, year after year, while people travel from all over the country (and sometimes the world) to celebrate the disappearance of three members of our family. It's this simple: We get it. We are reasonable people, and we understand why people are interested.

They aren't celebrating the deaths of Sarah, Bridget, and Margaret. That's not what this is about. People just love the unexplained. They love to be curious. They want to stand on the exact street where one of America's most notorious unsolved cases took place. They hate what happened to my aunts. Nobody in the year 2026 is saying that these girls got what they deserved. Well, maybe a few conspiracy-theory-peddling religious fanatics, but nobody in their right mind is celebrating their disappearances. It's October, people love spooky things this time of year, and there's nothing spookier than three teenage sisters vanishing without a trace from a small town nobody had ever heard of.

So, say we leave town—and then what? We are still Nancy and Iris Thornwick. Our names would still illicit a double take from anyone who hears them. Men would still be convinced we are actually witches and were put on this earth to ruin their lives. People would still whisper wherever we go. By staying in Westridge Cove, we are still the most talked about women in town, but at least we're able to pay our bills because of it. If you'd like to judge us for it, stand in line.

"Ladies and gentlemen, please have a seat. We just have a few quick, important items to go over, and then everyone can get back to their festival preparations."

Bucky Lancaster made the very bold choice to stray from his usual rotation of Brooks Brothers quarter-zips for a cream-colored cable-knit sweater. Maybe he saw all the Chris Evans thirst trap videos on social media and thought he could hop on the trend. He's not a bad looking older man; I just can't help but take into account the fact that he's an asshole while I'm appraising his appearance.

"We will have one small change in regard to this year's festivities," he begins, but his sentence is cut short when groans sound throughout the room.

"Okay, Butthole Bucky, we're firing them up early today, I see," I whisper to Lucy, and Mom kicks my ankle.

"Iris," she says through her teeth, holding onto that *s* for a good three seconds.

"Now calm down, everyone. The tourism industry is all about adapting to trends and trying to make each year's tourist season more successful than the last. In order to do that, we have to be open to change," Mayor Lancaster says, making a calming motion with his hands. As if that's ever worked, especially in a room that's mostly women.

"We don't mind change; we just want more of a heads up than the night before the crowds get here, Bucky!" yells Allen, owner of Transmissions Plus. "We tell you this every year."

"I don't think you're dealing with many tourists down at the mechanic's shop, Al," Lancaster counters.

"Bucky Lancaster, between the dead batteries, flat tires, and college kids who lock themselves out of their vehicles, every mechanic I have is on call twenty-four seven for the next month. Like everyone in this room, it's our busiest month of the year. I may not be in your tax bracket, but this month is my bread and butter, just like everyone else."

Mayor Bucky Lancaster has a large, Ivy-League vocabulary, but "sorry" and "I was wrong" are not in it. He simply responds by once again holding his palms in the air and muttering, "Alright, alright."

"The change is this. Each business in town is going to have a donation jar by the counter. We will be taking up collections to purchase a statue that will be placed in the town square to celebrate the lives of the Thornwick sisters.

Much like the *Bewitched* statue in Salem, it will be a tourist destination. Visitors will stand in line to get their pictures taken in front of Sarah, Bridget, and Margaret. We've found a sculptor out of Montreal to complete the piece and anticipate that with enough publicity, we can raise the funds by the end of October and have the piece completed by next fall. Any questions?"

I leap to my feet to tear this man a new asshole for doing this without our permission, when my mother grabs my arm and yanks me back into my folding chair. Lucy has gotten up to get a refill of the complimentary apple cider and donuts and sees this play out from across the room. She laughs so hard at Mom manhandling me, she spits a chunk of sugared dough right onto the floor in front of Miss Tilly from the Methodist church.

"I told him it was okay," Mom says through gritted teeth. "Sit your ass down."

I turn in my chair to look at her.

"You told him it was okay to have a sculpture of them in the middle of a park for everyone to gawk at?" I ask, incredulously.

"Iris, he shares in our desire to celebrate my sisters and their beautiful lives. He knew them, all three of them. He has no reason to want to disrespect their memories. I've seen this artist's work, and he really captures the beauty in his subjects. Maybe this will help people understand that these were three living, breathing girls who were loved very much, and the real tragedy is how they were treated by this town. May I remind you how supportive Bucky was when they went missing? He paid for the search party to continue after the state called it off. He's not the enemy you continue to paint him as, sweetheart."

Trying to get me to come around on my feelings about

Bucky Lancaster is like trying to convince me that my high school bully wasn't really that bad; I just misunderstood her intentions.

"I get where you're coming from, Mom. I'm sorry," I tell her, and it takes everything in me not to add that I'm sure he will find some way to benefit from this. Lancasters don't do anything for this town that doesn't directly benefit them or their rich friends somehow. There's something in it for him; I'm just not yet sure what it is.

Next, we get to the segment of the meeting where Steve Garbugli asserts his artistic integrity.

"Well," he starts, throwing the end of his mile-long fuchsia scarf over his right shoulder, "I was actually going to take a step back from participating in this blatant cash grab of a month, but I have decided my doors shall remain open every day in October, to help fund this beautiful sculpture to honor three of our own. We love you, Iris and Nancy. I hope we have procured a talented enough artist to capture the essence of your beautiful girls," he says, blowing us both a kiss. If the entire town wasn't watching, I would have blown that kiss right back with a middle finger attached to it. Instead, my mother and I place our hands over our hearts and mouth *thank you*, like we haven't both been sick of his shit since he opened the gallery twenty years ago.

The Herberts perform their yearly gesture of standing up to defend our family's honor but announce that since Mayor Lancaster has decided to raise funds for a statue in our family's honor, they don't have any issues, complaints, or suggestions this year. With our blessing, they retake their seats, satisfied that they have successfully defended our honor once again.

Well, that concludes this year's pointless pre-festival town hall meeting.

"Hold on everyone. We have one more announcement to make. Please give your attention to Chief Parker, and then everyone can be on their way," Bucky announces to the room, most of which have begun putting on their coats and making a mad dash for the remaining donuts.

Wally Parker saunters over to the podium. No longer in uniform, he's dressed in a red and black flannel with dark-wash jeans and his favorite boots. Well, I assume they are his favorite since he wears them so much. Not that I notice or care what the hell that man wears.

"Evening, everyone. Approximately three hours ago, my office received a call from the wife of Kellen DeYoung, who most of you know. Kellen didn't come home last night, which his wife Callie says is very unusual. Now, I'm sure Kellen is just off somewhere blowing off some steam, but as you know, we have large numbers of tourists descending on our little town, and for better or worse, Kellen is part of local lore because he was directly involved in the Thornwick case as a child. Has anyone had contact with Kellen DeYoung in the last twenty-four hours?" Wally asks, eyes searching the room. Not a single hand is raised.

Quiet but panicked chatter erupts around me. Kellen DeYoung has been a resident of Westridge Cove his entire life. He led a quiet life until he was thrust into the spotlight at the age of eight, when he was the first to accuse my aunts, his babysitters, of some pretty horrible things.

My relationship with Kellen has been rocky over the years. We both stayed in Westridge, so it has been impossible to avoid each other entirely, but I've done my best to look the other way when I see him in public. He works for Lancaster Enterprises, and in recent years has shown that he's just as horrible as the rest of the men employed there.

"Well, if anyone hears from him, please call the station

so we can put this matter to rest," Wally adds before leaving the podium.

I have to bite my cheeks so that I won't show even the hint of a smile. It's harder than you'd think.

I'm sure I'm succeeding until my eyes meet Lucy's from across the room, and she slowly shakes her head.

I jump to my feet. This is the perfect time to load up on fresh baked donuts while everyone's attention is on Bucky, who is giving his closing remarks. I grab two, wrap them in a napkin, and say goodbye to Mom on my way out. I wouldn't want anyone to stop me for small talk and notice that I'm not exactly concerned over Kellen DeYoung's whereabouts. I know exactly where he is.

Chapter Eleven

OCTOBER 29TH, 1993

The sisters woke up that Friday morning, got dressed for school, grabbed a quick breakfast, and joked with each other about the bizarre conversation they had with their mother the day before. None of them could have guessed that by the weekend, all hell would break loose.

After the girls' disappearance, that's what Sheila Thornwick would remember the most—how unserious they were when initially confronted about the allegations. They threw their heads back in laughter, roaring louder as each sister added another punchline to the conversation.

"It's probably because you spend all your time at Willow's Nook, trying to conjure up spirits and talking to ghosts—you're the reason we're getting accused of this. You and your witchcraft!" Bridget told Sarah, playfully slapping her hand like an old-school nun. "Shame on you."

"Me? Maggie is the one with a dream catcher hanging over her bed. Catching dreams is unnatural, and she should be banned from babysitting the sweet, innocent youth," Sarah retorted, barely getting the words out before she lost her composure.

"Girls," their mother said, slapping the table to get their attention. "This isn't funny. Do you know why those three boys down in West Memphis are sitting in jail as we speak? Because the town decided that they worshipped Satan, so they must be capable of killing those poor kids. Remember me telling you about the McMartin school case in California? Once one parent decided they were performing satanic rituals with their children, she convinced half the nation they were guilty without a shred of evidence. You girls need to take this seriously so we can nip it in the bud."

"I think it's supposed to be butt, Mom," Bridget offered.

That's when Sheila Thornwick lost her patience.

"Sarah, Bridget, Margaret, look at me. This is serious. These people are our friends and neighbors, and they are under the impression that you have involved their children in something nefarious. I know how ridiculous it sounds, but people believe crazy things when it comes to protecting their children. You know that this is a small town filled with good, church-going neighbors and if they think that you girls have gotten into something unholy, there's no telling what they'll try and do. After school tomorrow, you'll be stopping at each of their houses to explain yourselves. I mean it. I don't even know how I'm going to explain this to your father."

They apologized to their mother and went to their rooms, but only after they converged in Sarah's to discuss how absolutely ludicrous the situation was. They played a few sleepover games. The same games that teenage girls across America had been playing for years. What in the world was the issue?

.   .   .

The first to be confronted was Sarah, who laughed out loud when she was called a witch in the hallway on her way to first period. Next, Maggie opened her locker to find an upside-down cross taped to the inside. Finally, Bridget was cornered in the girls' restroom by two seniors who demanded to know what she "did to those little boys."

All three girls left school at lunch, deciding it was for the best after they were called names they didn't even understand.

"What in the hell is happening?" Maggie asked, cleaning the splattered mashed potatoes from her backpack. Someone flung them at her when she was leaving the lunchroom. "Amber Pantoni called me a child predator. What in the actual fuck?"

"Hey," called out Sarah's friend Noelle, jogging to catch up with the sisters on the edge of the parking lot. "What the fuck?"

"Yeah, we were just wondering the same," Sarah told her.

Noelle shook her head in disbelief, eyebrows pinched together, as she detailed all the rumors going around school.

They'd cut the boy's fingers so they could use their blood to conjure up the spirits of dead people. They'd sat in a circle and chanted until Maggie began to levitate. They had a magic book filled with spells. They'd lit candles, and the smoke turned different colors as they repeated their chants. They'd mixed potions together and forced the boys to drink them. The boys had lost all memory of the events that took place after they drank the magic potion. They'd said that the girls told them they'd be back on Saturday night to finish their ritual.

"You have to be kidding me," Bridget said, hands shaking. "None of that happened, and most of what you're describing happened in the movie we watched, *Hocus Pocus*. There's no way the kids said those things. They were probably just telling their parents about the movie and got confused."

It would be that simple: They'd march over to the Carters, followed by the DeYoung's and Chief Parker's house. They would explain what happened, and everyone would get a good laugh. Surely, nobody would believe that the Thornwick sisters were capable of harming children in any way, right?

Chapter Twelve

PRESENT DAY

October 1st in Westridge Cove is something you'd have to see to believe. I've never been one for crowds, and I'd never willingly partake in this madness, if I weren't getting paid very well for staying open for business.

This year I chose a Michael Myers mask for myself, and Mom is dressed as the Leprechaun, which is hilarious, given her height of five foot nothing. Wearing costumes is the only way we survive October. Nobody can gawk or harass us if they don't know who we are. We buy new ones to add to the rotation every November when they go on clearance after the holiday.

By now, we've heard it all. We are witches. We put curses on any man who crosses our paths. We kidnap children. We are out to get anyone who was involved in the accusations surrounding the sisters. Before they disappeared, they put a spell on us so we'd never be lucky in love —the jury is still out on that theory. There are even stories that we serve human remains at the café, yet this rumor only seems to increase business.

People are sick.

Today is the annual Witches of Westridge parade, aka the official kickoff of October in America's second most popular Halloween tourist town. That's right; last year we surpassed Sleepy Hollow and are second only to Salem, Massachusetts. Anytime another crime happens in our little community, it only increases business for the following year. Last fall was an eventful season for Wally and his officers, so we're expecting record numbers this year.

Mom and I let the employees handle the café during the parade so we can enjoy the festivities. We'll head to work afterward to help them out, as the after-parade rush gets crazier every year. Last October, we sold over one hundred slices of pumpkin pie in one night. We had to call Lenny down at the city dump to come empty our dumpsters a day early. This year, we rented an extra one for the entire month. Live and learn.

We make it to the end of Main Street just in time for the opening lines of "(Don't Fear) the Reaper" to begin. The morning after the disappearances, Sarah's Walkman was found in the middle of the alley behind Willow's Nook with a mixed cassette tape playing. It was documented in the police files that the Blue Oyster Cult hit was playing when the officer pressed stop, so it's become a major part of the lore surrounding their disappearances. It's now tradition to start the parade in front of Willow's Nook with the song blaring from the town's speakers, installed atop the lampposts. It used to drive my mother to tears, but over the years she's learned to embrace it. What a strange, strange life we live.

I reach into the pocket of my Michael Myers mechanic's jumpsuit and pull out my mini flask filled with bourbon. I'm typically not a big drinker, but getting through this month requires a little assistance. I turn to face Willow's store, hiding my face while I lift the mask to take a quick pull from the flask. There's a teenager I don't recognize working the checkout counter, so my eyes travel up above the store to Willow's apartment. She's standing in the window watching me take a swig. I wink as she shakes her head.

"Iris," my mom whispers, again drawing out the s a little too long at the end. I'm ready to be scolded when I turn to face her and she's holding out her hand, asking for a sip.

"Dang, Mom, I haven't seen you take a drink in years," I tell her, handing her the flask and covering her while she pulls her Leprechaun mask up. I snort when she flinches from the taste. Nancy Thornwick cannot handle her liquor, so I pull the flask back after her sip. "That'll be enough to take the edge off," I assure her.

As the warmth from the booze travels through our veins, we turn and put our masks back in place just in time to see a float with three women dancing in the middle, presumably dressed as the aunts. As they get closer, we see the names clearly printed on their shirts: Sarah, Bridget, Margaret. Mom gasps when she sees what they are holding—long spikes with severed heads on the ends. She's disgusted, but I love it.

"Who are the heads supposed to be?" Mom asks incredulously.

"Well, they all appear to be men, so my guess would be Chief Parker, Mr. Carter, and Mr. DeYoung," I reply, squinting to make out any identifying features on the heads. One of them has red spray-painted hair, so I'm assuming it's supposed to be Mr. Carter.

Mom gasps again when the float gets close enough to us to make out the small signs attached to each stick.

Carter.

Parker.

O'Conner?

"O'Conner?" Mom and I whisper in unison. Then it hits me. The newest theory by the internet sleuths. A kid named Dennis O'Conner let Sarah cheat off his test right before the girls disappeared. He reportedly asked her out on a date afterward and she blew him off. One of their class-mates came forward to recount the events, and someone in a Reddit thread found the interview in one of the police files that were made public. I explain this to Mom.

"Denny O'Conner? No, he was a good kid. He would never have had anything to do with what happened," Mom says, shaking her head.

"That's the thing with internet sleuths, Mom. They don't take the time to think about whether he was a good kid or not. They have one tiny piece of evidence that *might* point them in his direction, and they all foam at the mouth, thinking they are going to solve America's coldest case. There's no reasoning with them. I know their hearts are in the right place, but once they're on someone's trail, it's impossible to convince them otherwise."

"Do you ever go in these chat rooms?" she asks me.

I can't explain how precious it is to be asked this by a leprechaun who is struggling to stand in her pointy buckled shoes while holding her green top hat in place.

"Well, we don't really do chat rooms anymore, Mom. It's called Reddit, and yeah, sometimes I scroll around."

"Do you ever comment?"

Although she can't see me, I'm smiling under my mask.

"Only when I see rumors about us. I like to pretend I'm

a local with inside knowledge and add fuel to the fire. Just last week I commented that one of the cooks from the café went missing, and we are trying to keep it out of the news. You should have seen how excited everyone was to come get a sandwich and see if they can figure out what's going on."

"Iris Elizabeth, that's dishonest."

"Mom, it's called free advertising."

She tuts, but I can tell she sees my point, based on the lack of further argument. The crazier the rumors, the better it is for business. I don't make the rules. I even started one that the Thornwicks—Mom and me—were looking for another witch to add to our coven and were hoping to hand-pick one from the tourists this year. I had not anticipated how many aspiring witches there were on Reddit; the response was overwhelming.

We watch as the parade progresses into a more classic Halloween theme—ghosts, goblins, pumpkins, and the occasional witch with a black pointy hat. Everyone is having a good time and, surprisingly, that includes us. We've each taken another shot of bourbon so we're at that sweet spot, being just buzzed enough to think that the orange twinkly lights strung across Main Street from the light poles just might be the most magical we've ever seen. We are laughing at the kids dressed as munchkins from the *Wizard of Oz* and impressed by the intricate face paint on the zombies from the *Night of the Living Dead* float. Four men are dressed as ghouls and walking on stilts down the middle of Main Street, and their towering height is terrifying. *The Lost Boys* —that's the next float. There aren't any live actors in costumes on this one, just dummies tied to poles on each corner and dressed like the characters from the movies, complete with sunglasses and mullets.

"Where the hell are they getting these fake bodies?

They look way too real. I hate it," Mom says, her shoulders shivering while she nods toward the last float.

My attention goes to the three guys standing in front of us on the curb when one of them says my name. I turn to Mom and shake my head, reminding her not to engage.

"Yeah, bro, but have you seen Iris Thornwick? She's hot as hell. I'd risk a curse to hit that any day of the week," Bro Number One boasts.

"I read on Facebook that she normally works the lunch shift. Let's pop in tomorrow. I'll have her number before we leave; she looks easy," Bro Number Two chimes in.

"Did you see her mom, though? Like fine wine, gentlemen. She has unresolved sister trauma, and that's almost as good as daddy issues."

This comment by none other than Bro Number Three, combined with the two pulls of bourbon, inspires my leg to rise a few feet off the ground and kick him from behind, causing his knees to buckle before I've had time to think it through. He falls forward into the street before quickly picking himself up and spinning to face us.

"What's your problem, man?"

"Don't look at us," I say in a deep voice, holding my hands in the air and then pointing to my right. By some sort of dumb luck, there's a group of teenagers running away from us. The perfect suspects.

The injured bro lunges as if he's going to chase after them, before one of his fellow bros holds a stiff arm in front of his chest to stop him.

"Not worth it, man. Not worth it."

They turn back around to watch the remainder of the parade, and my satisfaction is cut short when I remember my mother was next to me to witness the whole interaction. Nancy Thornwick knows her daughter has a smart mouth, but she's never seen me display a hint of violence toward anyone.

"Nobody talks about my mother like that," I whisper through the small ear hole in her green rubber mask.

Her hand rises to rub my back and squeeze my shoulder. I'm sure she sees this as a very rare lapse in judgement made by her sweet and well-behaved daughter, and only because she was defending her mom's honor.

If she only knew the things that I've done and, even worse, what I have planned.

Chapter Thirteen

OCTOBER 29TH, 1993

Meeting with the boys' parents was a colossal shitshow, to put it mildly. The sisters waited until shortly after 5:00 p.m. on Friday, when everyone would be home from work, so they could make the rounds and explain themselves. All three sisters believed it would be a quick conversation: They'd detail the games they were playing, the movie they watched with the kids, and apologize for any confusion. Hopefully, they'd all share a good laugh, and the families would plan for the girls' next babysitting shift.

First was the Carter family. The girls arrived at the scene of the crime—the house where the alleged "satanic rituals" took place. When they entered the house after being invited in by Mr. Carter, Sarah noticed a copy of *Michelle Remembers* on the coffee table next to a leather-bound copy of the bible and thought *Oh, shit. Here we go.* Her sisters may not be familiar with the book, but Willow Nora told her all about it. A woman's outrageous and unbelievable account of being sold to a satanic cult by her parents—it was widely considered to be the match that ignited the satanic panic in the eighties. Despite her claims being debunked and the controversy after she married the psychologist she co-authored the book with, many took her words as gospel. For the last decade or so, anyone seen as "different," especially in small towns, was suddenly accused of worshipping Satan. Oh, you listen to Judas Priest? You like to wear black? I didn't see you in church last Sunday? *Boom*—Satanist. Case closed. People were so damned scared by the things they didn't understand; it was easier to just condemn them than to spend five minutes of their precious time trying to gather more information.

At first, the girls were optimistic. Mr. Carter invited them to sit in the living room. He appeared to be listening intently to their explanation, although the girls also suspected he was simply ready to be done with this ridiculous situation and was welcoming any sort of resolution that didn't require his further involvement. It was the weekend, and he had golf to play and Manhattans to drink.

"You've always been such good girls. I'm sure this is all a misunderstanding that will blow over. You all need to just calm down and let the adults handle it."

All sense of rationality went out the window when Carol Carter arrived home from her Junior League meeting.

"Are you kidding me? Why are these devil-worshipping little sluts in our home?" she shouted, throwing her purse on the entryway table.

Maggie flinched at the word *sluts*. At just fifteen years old, she'd heard the word used playfully by friends and derogatorily in plenty of movies, but never in a negative way aimed *at* her. It seemed like such a dirty, adult word. She hated it. It felt as if she had been slapped. What had she done to deserve this?

"Mrs. Carter, if you would just—" Sarah began.

"If I would just what?" Carol Carter interrupted her. "Allow you a little more time with our precious children so you can finish your rituals? You didn't quite get to the part where you snatched their souls right out of their bodies or kidnapped one of them for your sacrifice; did we come home too early and interrupt you?"

Too early? You came home after midnight hammered as hell and offering us money for staying late, Bridget thought but didn't say it out loud. The kids were asleep when the parents arrived; did they think the girls tucked them into their sleeping bags after teaching them how to worship the devil?

"This is all a big misunderstanding. We would never—"

"You," Carol cut Maggie off. "You, Margaret Thornwick, are the one I thought better of. I never imagined you'd be capable of this. Your mother must be so ashamed."

As she spoke, she motioned toward Maggie's outfit—a blue button-down shirt with a white V-neck sweater over it. Her brown penny loafers completed the outfit, making her look more like a preppy teen vacationing on Nantucket, rather than a child-sacrificing Satanist.

"Because she's *not* capable of this. None of us are. We were just playing stupid games," Bridget argued. "The boys watched *Hocus Pocus* with us and must have had bad dreams or gotten confused. Half of the things they are accusing us of are straight from the movie. We played *Light as a Feather, Stiff as a Board,* and the boys must've thought Maggie was really levitating. It was just a silly game."

"Oh, I bet you couldn't wait to show him that horrible movie so you could normalize witchcraft in the eyes of innocent children. Did Willow Nora give you some tips? Did you drug them before or after you pressed play?"

Sarah scoffed loudly. She always got defensive when Willow was criticized in any way. Bridget found it odd that Sarah somehow remained calm while being personally attacked alongside her younger sisters, but she drew the line at her strange old lady friend's name being brought into the discussion.

"First of all, it's a Disney movie. As in Walt-Fucking-Disney. Second of all, are you accusing us of witchcraft or satanic worship here? They are two very different things, Carol. Third, weren't you the one dressed as Satan that night? You know, when you came home three sheets to the wind with your horns on sideways?" Sarah shouted and Maggie's eyes grew wide. They never spoke to adults like that; their parents taught them better. Not only was she being combative and cussing, but she called Mrs. Carter by her first name. Their mother would shit a brick if she knew.

Sarah's hands were shaking as she continued. "We watched your children, who were horribly behaved by the way, and let them watch a Disney movie before bed. They woke up while we were playing stupid sleepover games and we let them join in. That's it. No witchcraft, no devil worshipping, nothing strange. We've been watching those boys for years, and you've never had an issue. This is ridiculous."

"What's ridiculous is that you three just ruined your futures in one night. I hope it was worth it," Carol said, crossing her arms over her chest.

Ruined our futures? Maggie thought. This was getting so incredibly blown out of proportion, her head was spinning. They hadn't done anything wrong. They were just kids themselves.

"I think you should go," Mr. Carter added, barely above a whisper. They knew he didn't completely agree with his wife, or he wouldn't have been so cordial when he invited them in. Like most men in Westridge Cove, he just wanted to keep the peace at home, so it wasn't another source of stress in his world of board meetings and corporate presentations.

The girls were fired up on the walk to the next house to speak to Mr. and Mrs. DeYoung, but that shock switched to devastation when Keith DeYoung answered the door and refused to allow the girls inside, ordering them to leave his house immediately.

"I can't believe we trusted you girls with our children. Barrett hasn't slept a wink; he's traumatized," Keith told them. His hands were practically throbbing, balled into fists at his side. "You need to leave now and sort out whatever demons you've invited into your lives."

Karen DeYoung was in the kitchen shouting something about holy water and judgement day. If the events weren't all so crazy, this whole situation would be comical.

They walked in near silence to Chief Parker's house a few blocks away. After knocking several times and waiting to hear footsteps, they concluded he must be at work.

"Should we walk to the station?" Bridget asked.

"Might as well. He's our last hope of any adult in this damn situation having a lick of sense," Sarah added.

"How could these people believe we would do something like this?" Maggie asked, and it broke both of her older sisters to see the pain in her eyes. "They've known us our entire lives. We've taken good care of their kids."

The police station was a ten-minute walk from the DeYoung home. Roughly two minutes into the walk, it began to snow. The first snow of the season was always

Sarah's favorite. Big, fat flakes landing on the vibrantly colored leaves; everywhere she turned she saw a scene that could be on the cover of one of those nature calendars her mom purchased every year for the front of the refrigerator. Her stomach ached so badly from the predicament they were in, she couldn't even find joy in the beauty of the snowfall.

"It all feels like a big prank, right? Like these people got together and came up with the most obscene, unbelievable things they could accuse us of and then convinced half the town that it was all true. I just can't believe this is happening," Bridget said, her Converse sneakers leaving footprints bearing the company's logo in the freshly fallen snow.

"Hey, we'll laugh about this someday. I promise," Sarah told her, stopping on the sidewalk to face her sisters. They all halted and faced each other, realizing it was the first time they'd really looked into each other's eyes all day. Sarah reached both her hands out and held her sisters' with a tight grip. "Willow taught me that people can be so ugly, especially when they see you as different. We just need to convince these people that we're not actually strange; we just babysat a few kids with wild imaginations who started silly rumors about us. That's all."

They were startled by the shrill horn of a passing car.

"Now they're casting a spell in the middle of Tenth Street!" a boy yelled from the passenger window. "Go to hell, witches!"

The girls looked down at their hands, which were each holding that of their sisters while they stood in a circle on the sidewalk of one of Westridge Cove's busiest streets.

"Honestly, we set ourselves up for that one," Maggie said, forcing a smile.

The sisters attempted to do the same, but the smiles that started at their lips never quite made it to their eyes.

They made it to the police station just as the snowfall seemed to ramp up into fat, floating flakes, and Chief Rex Parker was exiting through the side door, headed toward his patrol car.

"Chief Parker," Maggie yelled.

Rex turned on his heels and raised his hand to wave, but his smile and his arm fell when he saw who was calling his name. He let out a low whistle.

"You girls have got yourself in some shit. Pardon my language, but, you have. Theresa said she's been fielding calls all day from parents, worried that you three have involved their kids in some sort of witchcraft. Most of them were kids you've never even babysat before. It's mass hysteria; what the hell do you girls have to say for yourselves?"

Sarah stepped forward first, breaking the usual routine of Maggie being the voice of reason in these situations.

"Chief Parker, you know us. We would never be into that kind of stuff. Didn't you ask Wally? The kids had a good time and then we put them to bed. These accusations are insane."

Parker removed his hat and held it in his hands like a sheriff from an old western movie. "Now, girls, you know I wouldn't take the word of a six-year-old when investigating a possible crime. It's not about testimony from four little boys."

A lightbulb went off in Bridget's head.

"That's it—Ann! Ann Haven was there with us. You can call her and she'll tell you everything."

She couldn't believe the girls didn't think of it sooner, but the last forty-eight hours had been absolute pandemonium. It slipped the girls' minds that Ann was even there during the time they were accused of witchcraft, Satanism, or whatever else the locals would like to tack onto the list of offenses.

"I can give you her number," Sarah offered.

"No need," Rex replied. "Why don't you girls follow me?"

He led them through a locked side door of the police station and down a narrow hall to what they assume was an interrogation room, not unlike the ones they've seen in movies. He motioned for them to sit before he leaned forward and rolled a black cart toward them with a VCR and small television perched on top. He started the tape and began to fast forward, looking for a certain spot in the recording.

The girls sat silent as they saw their friend Ann Haven on the screen, sitting at the very table they were currently leaning their elbows on.

Rex pressed stop and then play. The girls couldn't see him in the recording, but they recognized his voice off-screen.

"So, you're saying these boys are telling the truth, Ann?"

Without emotion, she lifted her head and appeared to stare directly at him before responding.

"It's all true, Chief Parker. It was horrible."

Chapter Fourteen

PRESENT DAY

By the time Mom and I make it back to the café, our bourbon buzzes have worn off, and we're additionally sobered by the sight from the sidewalk. There isn't an open parking spot in the entire lot, a line of people has formed out the door and around the corner of the building, and there's a server out back by the dumpster crying.

"You hop in and help the hostess handle the wait list, and I'll talk Nikki down from the ledge," I tell Mom. She smiles briefly before pulling her mask down and turning to go inside, and I know what she's thinking—that her daughter is just like her little sister, Maggie. She's told me this my entire life. Despite being the youngest sister, Maggie was always the one to stay calm and take charge. I must have inherited these qualities from her because Mom says I've been behaving this way since the second grade, when I took charge of the school play after Joey Johnson shouted cuss words into the microphone, causing Mrs. Nelson to have a panic attack.

Nikki wipes beneath her eyes in a swift motion when she sees me approaching. It appears she's been crying so furiously that her chest and neck are covered in red splotches.

"Sorry, Iris, I was just taking a quick smoke break."

"You don't smoke, Nikki."

Her cheeks redden. As she prepares another excuse, I open my arms to pull her into a hug. I'm sure there are a lot of management advice books that would strongly caution you to not hug your employees, but the authors are only familiar with corporate America and not small-town cafés owned by a mother and daughter team who grew up alongside nearly every employee they've ever hired. Well, we've now graduated to hiring the *children* of people we grew up with, but you get the gist.

"Look at me," I tell her, pulling out of the hug and placing a hand on each shoulder. "You know we only cry in the walk-in cooler. I have no choice but to write you up for showing emotion outdoors."

She laughs. Jackpot. That's all you really need to get the ball rolling. Laughter. And then they'll remember to breathe. And once they breathe, you can help ground them and make them realize it's not that serious.

"Let me ask you this: Are you hurt?"

"No, ma'am."

"Don't call me ma'am. That's my mother. Okay, did somebody die?"

"No."

"Has your dog been kidnapped by evil criminals demanding a ransom that you cannot pay?"

"I don't have a dog."

"Okay, then whatever it is—it's not that bad. Whenever I feel like crying or screaming or throwing something during a shift, I like to remember a few things. First, it's only food. That's all. It's not that serious. None of this will matter tomorrow. Second, if a customer is being horrible to you, it always has more to do with them than it does with you. They are probably very miserable in their lives, and their only sense of satisfaction comes from belittling a nineteen-year-old waitress at a café. What a sad life that is, eh?"

Nikki nods but doesn't respond. I can tell from the recognition in her eyes that it was absolutely a customer who upset her.

"And if it's an employee who made you cry, just tell me who it was, and I'll chop them up and hide their body in the freezer until after the rush because you're my favorite server and I'd do that for you. Don't tell the others. Now, are you ready to go back inside?"

She inhales deeply and nods. It takes me by surprise when she grabs *my* shoulders and pulls me in for a hug that is so tight, I nearly lose my breath.

"Thank you, Iris," she whispers in my ear. "You always know what to say. Sorry I lost my shit. I'm good now."

I pull away and straighten the fairy wings on her costume.

"The good news is that your Tinkerbell outfit is adorable, so your tips are going to be ridiculous, and also, remember that this shift has to end eventually. I remind myself of that nearly every day. We close at ten, so there's only so many hours in the day that these bastards can terrorize us with snapping fingers, requests for ranch, and belittling comments about waiting tables for a living."

"I wish the money wasn't so good this month," she says with a shrug.

"You and me both, Nikki. You and me both."

I won't disrespect our armed forces by saying that

walking into the restaurant is like walking into a war zone, but it's just what comes to mind as I swing the back door open.

The walk-in cooler door is swung wide open, which immediately makes me want to strangle someone. Luckily, the temperature reading is still well within range, so it appears that it wasn't open for long. I close the door and head toward the cook line, which has every station manned and an extra guy on the fryers, because tourists sure do love their boneless wings and mozzarella sticks.

The ticket printer is spitting out new orders at such a rapid rate, I know I'll hear that sound in my nightmares tonight. There isn't a clean apron in sight. Every employee I have in the back is covered by flour, batter, sauce, or a combination of all three. The best expo I have, Holly, is working to assemble and garnish all the plates before the servers or food runners take them out. This is the closest I've seen her come to looking flustered; she normally has nerves of steel.

"Holly, I'm here," I tell her as I grab a clean apron from the linen pile. "Talk to me; where we at?"

"Table thirty-one just needs one more chef salad, and it's ready to go; table twenty needs garnishes and dressings; table five needs garnishes and whipped cream on their desserts; and holy shit—when has the craziness ever began this early? It's only the first of the month, for Christ's sakes."

I grab the salad for table thirty-one and hand the full tray to a food runner.

"Let's get through the shift, and then we can talk about how fucking crazy this is," I tell her, reaching in front of her for an empty ramekin before filling it with French dressing.

"There's no way we make it through the week without a delivery," she says, and I notice her hand is shaking. "We're going to run out of everything." If I weren't getting my ass kicked, I'd smile. This is it. We are finally busy enough to make Holly lose her cool. It only took a few years.

"Yep, I'll call our rep after we close and leave him a message. He knows he's on call for a hot-shot truck all month. It'll be okay. Everything will be okay. It's just food."

"God, you're good at this," she mumbles. With renewed energy, she starts tackling all the orders on the slips in front of her with the precision of someone who could do this job in their sleep. I smile. I may be good at calming people during times of stress, but damn if she isn't good at what she does, as well.

Selfishly, I'm annoyed at Lucy for not being here. She was the best server we've ever had, and she'd have this place running like a well-oiled machine. Instead, she's probably off having the time of her life since she no longer works in a business that gets rocked the entire month of October. I know it's not her fault, but I still leave myself a mental reminder to throat punch her when I see her next. And if she's currently sitting in the dining room of my restaurant enjoying a nice meal while I get my ass handed to me, it will be a double throat punch.

Once Holly has the tickets under control, I take off my apron, pull my mask back down, and make my way to the front of the restaurant to check on the employees and see what I can do to help. I've found that my best plan of action when we're this busy, and I'm not working as a server myself, is to make my rounds and see what I can get for the customers while their server is busy. I make a game of chanting everything on the list to myself as I walk back to the kitchen. It's silly, but it works.

Side of ranch, Diet Coke, extra napkins.
Side of ranch, Diet Coke, extra napkins.

I'm sure the sight of a pint-sized Michael Myers mumbling these things is just as ridiculous as it sounds, but I can't risk taking off my mask when we're this busy. None of the tourists know that Iris and Nancy Thornwick are working this shift, and I'd like to keep it that way. In fact, not a single tourist will see our faces all month if I have anything to say about it.

I've got the side of ranch in one hand, and the other hand is wrapped around a cup being filled with ice when I hear the unmistakable squawk of a police radio. My stomach drops, before I remind myself that I've been preparing every detail of my crimes for months. Every scenario has repeated through my mind on a loop; there's no way I've made a foolish mistake this early in the game. But no matter how many times I've reassured myself of this, doubt still seems to creep into my anxious mind.

I sharply turn my head at the sound of the radio and see two Westridge Public Safety officers sitting at the bar. After calming my nerves and convincing myself they aren't here for me, I chase away the feeling of being disappointed that Wally isn't with them.

Every head in the restaurant turns as the two men throw some cash on the counter, wipe their faces with napkins, and rush out the door to their police cruiser. Well, every head except for mine because I'm sure I know where they are headed.

Chapter Fifteen

PRESENT DAY

Although Lucy wisely kept her distance while we continued to get bombarded with hungry tourists until closing time, she's here now, helping me sweep under the tables and restock the condiments, so I can sleep for a few hours and then get rocked again tomorrow.

"Is this the busiest we've ever been?" she asks, leaning on the wooden handle of her broom.

"We? *We?*" I ask, rapidly motioning between the two of us. "Who the fuck is 'we,' Lucy Goosey?"

"Okay, my bad. But I did walk by and see how busy you were and decided to give you your space. I know how cranky you get when you're that slammed."

She's right. It was best she stayed away, particularly during shift change when I fantasized about strangling several employees and a handful of customers.

"Yes, to answer your question. I haven't run the final numbers yet, but Mom says she thinks it's the busiest Thursday we've ever had. I can't imagine what the rest of this month is going to be like or how we're going to handle it."

"You will. You always do," she assures me.

"I'm not sure how my skin is going to recover from wearing masks all month, I'm already starting to break out and—"

My words are cut off by the sound of a breaking news alert on the TV hanging over the breakfast counter. One of the servers comes from the kitchen and grabs the remote, turning the volume up when she sees our local reporter, Sophia Smith, broadcasting from in front of the Thornwick Witch Museum.

"This is Sophia Smith, coming to you live from Westridge Cove where a body was found early this evening by a local resident while cleaning up from this morning's parade. The deceased's name will not be released until next of kin is notified, but the WKTV newsroom has confirmed that authorities have identified the victim. When we reached out to the department's spokesperson to ask if the public is at risk, she only advised that residents and tourists remain vigilant as always. This story is still developing, and we will be back with further details as we receive them. Now, back to Jonathan at the news desk for more local stories and weather."

Lucy snaps her head in my direction, furrowing her brows with an accusatory stare. I continue sweeping the tiles until the several employees who were gathered in front of the television move back to the kitchen to finish their closing duties.

"Why do you always assume I have something to do with these things?" I whisper to her, sweeping the straw wrappers and cracker crumbs into the dustpan.

"Because of your recent interest in becoming Westridge

Cove's resident homicidal maniac," she responds, her lips forming a tight line. She cocks her head as if to say *Well, can you argue with that?* But I simply shrug.

A few light taps on the locked entryway door steal my attention. Preparing to deal with an intoxicated tourist who disregarded the CLOSED sign, I spin in the direction of the door, wearing a scowl. My expression loosens when I see Wally Parker's face in the window. He holds up his index finger, signifying this will only take a minute. My jaw tightens when I remember that this will be the man investigating the murder I just committed.

Propping my broom against the counter, I hurry to the door, unlatching the metal lock before ushering him in.

"I hear you're having a busy night, Parker," I tell him, and I can feel Lucy staring a hole through the back of my head. There will never be a day that Lucy betrays me, but it doesn't mean she agrees with all of my decisions. I'd bounced the idea of killing Kellen off of her a few times, but I don't think she believed I was serious.

"You don't know the half of it, Thornwick," he responds, walking to the breakfast counter and leaning on both hands to support his weight. To the residents of Westridge, he's a stoic, unflappable hero who keeps our town safe, but I know Wally a lot better than that. He may put on a brave face, but having an unsolved crime in his community is his biggest fear. He sees himself as a failure when it happens. Believe what you want, but I do feel an incredible amount of guilt for being the reason he might not solve the crimes that occur in our community this year.

He turns his head in both directions and then leans toward me before telling me what happened. Lucy pretends to be busy filling the saltshakers; she knows she doesn't need to eavesdrop because I'll tell her everything the minute he leaves.

"Iris, it's pretty bad. It's Kellen DeYoung. He was murdered."

I place my hand over my heart as I gasp and then instantly regret it, wondering if it was too much. You can't oversell the lies; that's how you get caught.

"Are you sure it wasn't suicide? I heard he and Callie were having issues and he wasn't himself lately."

"Oh, we're sure. It was like something out of a horror movie. Everyone was breaking down the floats from the parade when they found him. The vampire float—the one that had the dummies dressed up as Dracula and whatnot? Well, someone propped his body up alongside the fake ones. While we were searching for Kellen, his body was being paraded in front of thousands of people and nobody knew it was him. He had an axe sticking out of his head and everyone thought it was a prop. When the internet finds out about this, they are going to go nuts. I've got to get some leads by the time that happens."

I gasp again, this one more reserved. I silently applaud myself.

"Oh my God, Wally, that's horrible. Do they think it was a tourist? Maybe someone obsessed with the case? You know as well as I do that these internet weirdos blame us kids for what happened."

Wally knows all too well. Even though he never accused my aunts of anything that night, he still received a few threats when the case picked up momentum again in recent years.

"It could be. Or hell, it could be a local he pissed off. He works for Bucky, and that man has no shortage of enemies. I don't know, Iris. I'm grasping at straws here. We've got nothing."

I tap my pointer finger on my chin while I stare out the café's large window, mentally counting to five before I deliver my planned line.

"Wait, you said the vampire float? You mean the *Lost Boys* themed one? That was the float I saw them working on in the alley behind Ann Haven's house last week when I was on my morning walk. Her boutique sponsored it. You don't think . . . Surely Ann wouldn't have had anything to do with Kellen's death, right? Maybe she was worried he was starting to remember things from his childhood, and she wanted to shut him up."

God bless him, he acts like this could be it; it could be the lead that cracks this case wide open. I pour him what's left in our coffee carafe, and he takes the disposable cup without waiting for me to put a lid on it. "Thanks, Iris. I'll catch up with you tomorrow," he shouts on his way out the door.

Once he's in his police cruiser, Lucy joins me at the counter.

"An axe in his head, Iris? A fucking axe? How the hell did that happen?"

I resume my sweeping and answer her with a shrug.

"Well, I put it there, silly."

Chapter Sixteen

OCTOBER 30TH, 1993

s if it didn't already seem like some sort of cruel town-wide joke being played on the Thornwick sisters, they were now reeling from the news that their friend Ann Haven was the only witness over the age of eight who gave a statement accusing them of something so ridiculous and sinister.

"I called twice last night and once this morning. I left messages on her answering machine, and she still hasn't called back," Sarah said.

All three girls were lying on their backs on the floor of Bridget and Maggie's room, staring at the ceiling. Maggie periodically slapping Sarah's hand each time she drummed her nails on the hardwood floor, a nervous tic that drove her insane.

"It just doesn't make any fucking sense. Why would she lie? Do you think they tricked her somehow?" Bridget asked.

"Maybe they starved her and wouldn't give her any

water until she started to lose her mind and gave a false confession so they'd let her out of there," Maggie offered, propping herself up on her elbows.

"Westridge Public Safety using torture tactics on a teenage girl? I mean, I guess I wouldn't put it past them," Sarah responded.

"What the fuck are we going to do? We don't even know what exactly we are being accused of," Bridget said, this time climbing to her feet and beginning to pace.

A loud *thwack* steals their attention, seemingly coming from outside the house. Bridget rushed to the window just in time to see four more eggs being pelted at the front door by two perpetrators in black ski masks. They took off, running down the street before hopping in a Chevy Blazer and peeling away.

The girls ran down the stairs and out the front door to investigate, but Sheila Thornwick was already on the front porch assessing the damage.

"What is happening?" she asked, a horrified look on her face. "This is getting entirely too out of hand. I'm calling Rex Parker."

"And what is he going to do? He told us yesterday that Ann Haven is the reason we're being investigated. Why would she lie about us?" Maggie asked. When Sheila saw the devastation and fear in Maggie's eyes, she hurried in her direction and wrapped her arms around her youngest daughter.

There was no need for their mother to call Chief Parker. His cruiser pulled in the driveway just moments later. He exited the driver's door, fidgeted with his radio and belt a few times, and made his way to the front of the house, stopping short when he saw the egg yolks running down the blue siding of the house. He shook his head and simply said, "Girls, let's go inside. We need to talk."

They all nodded, and Sheila led the way, but not before offering to throw on a pot of coffee, the universal Midwest gesture during a stressful gathering. They all took seats around the dinner table as Sheila, with shaking hands, prepared the grounds for the coffee maker.

"Peter working shutdown?" Rex asked, looking around the room. Each girl nodded. "Sheila, as their parent, do I have your verbal consent to ask the girls a few questions?"

Sheila glanced at her daughters and agreed to his request, receiving no opposition from the girls. It was a strange feeling for them all, much like being sent to the principal's office when they hadn't done anything wrong. It obviously seemed much more serious now that law enforcement was involved, but it was that same panic that maybe they had accidentally broken some sort of rule they weren't aware of.

"May I ask what exactly we are being accused of?" Maggie asked, ever the one to take charge and ask the tough questions.

"Well, girls; I'm going to be honest with you. The circumstances seem to have changed in the last few hours. I'm sure you've heard the rumors: witchcraft, spells, dark magic—you get the gist."

Again, if it weren't all so devastating, it would be ridiculous enough to laugh. The girls were in no mood to see humor in the situation anymore.

When they didn't respond, he continued.

"One of the parents called me this morning with some additional accusations after having more conversations with the boys. We called Ann Haven in for further questioning, and as you now know she corroborated the details of their story. She said she didn't come forward on her own because she feared for her life and didn't know what you girls were capable of."

"This can't really be happening," Sheila said, setting an empty mug in front of Rex. "Ann has been a friend of the girls since they were little. Why would she do this? What in the world are they being accused of now?"

"Well, Sheila, Ann spun quite the story when we brought her in this morning. She had a hoarse voice and said the girls cast a spell of sickness on her," he said, pulling a small notebook out of his front pocket to reference. "She said she was feeling worse by the minute and knew that it was the girls who did it to punish her for talking to me the day before. That's a direct quote."

"Cast a spell? Cast. A. Spell. Rex, you've known my girls their entire lives. Are you hearing yourself?"

Rex hung his head momentarily before shaking it and raising his chin to match Sheila's gaze.

"Sheila, you need to know, I'm just doing my job. I have to get to the bottom of this, and that means questioning your girls. Between you and me, of course these accusations seem even more preposterous when I say them out loud, but I've got a mob of angry residents at my office door, demanding answers. I'm just doing my due diligence. I assure you, this isn't fun for me, either. I've got a son and I can't afford to lose this job, but the community will force me out of office if I don't find a resolution to all of this nonsense."

"By all means, Rex," Sheila began, walking over to pour from the carafe of freshly brewed Folgers, "please continue to question my teenage daughters about using witchcraft to give their friend a sore throat."

Rex jumped back when Sheila *accidentally* overflowed his ceramic mug, adorned with geese wearing blue bonnets.

Black liquid sloshed over the edge of the mug and hit the table before splashing onto his hand.

"Whoops, did you want me to leave you room for cream?"

Maggie watched her mother smirk and shrug and thought, *My mother, the badass.*

"It's not just about Ann's sore throat," Rex began, after retrieving a napkin to blot the splattered coffee in front of him. "She said the girls were having the kids read from some sort of book they brought with them. She said they took a lock of hair from each of the kids. They were doing chants and told the boys they'd be back to get them on Devil's Night to complete the spell. As you know, that's tonight. The parents are worried sick that the girls are going to try and snatch those boys up."

Devil's Night, aka the night before Halloween, was a popular night in the Midwest for juvenile shenanigans, like toilet papering houses and smashing pumpkins. This was the first the girls had heard of an additional tradition of snatching up adolescent boys to use for witchcraft. They *had* discussed their plans for Devil's Night before this—to make a batch of popcorn, pick up pumpkin-flavored milkshakes from the Dairy Barn, and watch Christian Slater host *Saturday Night Live* while they worked on the final touches of their Halloween costumes. Sarah laughed to herself and shook her head, remembering the costumes Sheila made them from the black fabric she picked up at JoAnne's the week before. The three Thornwick sisters were planning on being witches for Halloween. Oh, the irony.

"Well, Chief Parker, I think our official statement would be that no, we did not cast a spell on our friend that we've known since the second grade, we don't own any sort of witchcraft or satanic books, we didn't cut off locks of anyone's hair, and we have nothing on our agenda tonight that would involve kidnapping young children," Bridget said, shaking her head at the absurdity of the statement.

"Do you have any idea why Ann would say these things? Did any of you girls have a falling out with her? Any reason she'd be seeking revenge against you?"

The girls wracked their brains. The last time any of them had an argument with Ann was probably in the eighth grade when she kissed Tony Olson at the Snowball dance, despite knowing that Sarah had a crush on him. They had fun with her Wednesday night, watching *Candyman* and then playing their stupid games—most of which were Ann's idea. She was in a perfectly normal mood when she left the house, shortly before the parents arrived to relieve the girls. Sarah even asked if she wanted to go to the theater and watch the *Nightmare Before Christmas* the following week, and Ann sounded excited about it.

"Chief Parker, you saw the boys that night. You brought Wally home. Did any of them seem like they had just witnessed us performing any sort of witchcraft? Satanic rituals? Casting spells? Did they appear to fear for their lives because we had promised to come back and get them the night before Halloween? Were any of them missing a chunk of hair?"

Rex shook his head. "Wally fell asleep in the car, and I had to carry him in the house. He acted completely normal at breakfast the next morning and when I dropped him off at school. I was just as shocked as you girls when Carol Carter called me. I didn't want to press Wally too hard, so I asked him if he had fun at the Carters' house and he lit up, telling me about watching scary movies and eating pizza. He had nothing strange to say."

"What else can my daughters do to clear their names? To prove this is all a misunderstanding and that the boys obviously have active imaginations and got these ideas from a silly movie they all watched?"

Sarah sighed, thinking of the urban legends she believed when she was that age. She remembered when all the kids were convinced that Mr. Pearson, the elementary school counselor, ate cats for dinner. One of the boys in her class started the rumor that he was breaking into the animal shelter at night and stealing them for his stew. Everyone believed it. Sarah was terrified of Mr. Pearson until a few years later, in middle school, when that same boy admitted he'd made up the rumor because he was bored.

"Well, Sheila, my next stop is Nancy's house. With her permission, I'd like to ask Iris a few questions about what she may have seen or heard when her aunts babysat her on Wednesday night."

"Yes, please, let's involve yet another six-year-old when it comes to the validity of these accusations against my daughters. Don't forget to question the pet cat; he was there, too. Maybe he was a coconspirator; you better prepare a very small set of handcuffs in case you need to take him in."

"Sheila, please," Rex began, but Sheila simply held up a palm in his direction.

"Rex, just do your damn job and clear their names so we can move on. This has gotten out of hand, and I want it done."

It was the first and last time the girls heard their mother use such language. It's amazing how out of character someone can act when they are protecting the ones they love.

Chapter Seventeen

PRESENT DAY

I'm about to turn off the lights and lock up the café when the phone mounted on the kitchen wall rings; a sound so shrill and unexpected, it makes my heart skip a beat.

"Thornwick Café, this is Ir— Elizabeth. How can I help you?"

A long exhale on the other end.

"Iris, I know it's you. It's Willow."

Willow Nora, the Widow Nora of Winston Street
All her life they thought she was so damn sweet
Until she killed her husband and she cooked him in
the meat
So hide your kids from the Widow of Winston Street

Leave it to children to create the most ridiculous and cruel rhymes, without once thinking of the hurt they're causing. Mom tells me that Aunt Sarah used to go ham on anyone who recited the chant; she was Willow's biggest defender.

"Hey, Willow, you just caught me. I was about to lock up. Is everything okay?" I ask.

"Yes, dear, but would you mind stopping by quickly on your way home, or do you have big plans to go out on the town and hunt down some swinging dicks?"

I smile.

"I can push those plans back an hour or so; the dicks will still be there. Do you need me to pick anything up for you on my way?"

"I'm not a damn invalid Iris. I just need to speak with you. Just come over."

I'm going to miss her smart mouth when she's gone.

She's got to be damn near eighty years old by now. By the way my mom tells it, Willow seemed elderly back when they were young. I'm not completely sold on dark magic or witchcraft, but something has kept her looking the same for decades, and I don't believe it's skin cream.

I hang up the phone and look at Lucy, who is standing by the back door and tapping her foot, ready to lock up with me and leave.

"Hey, why don't you go ahead and go to the Alibi and I'll meet you there? I've gotta swing by Willow's real quick."

She gives me a sympathetic look but knows better than to argue. That woman meant the world to at least one of my aunts and was incredibly supportive of Mom after she lost her sisters. The least I can do is entertain her wacky requests once in a while, like only using landline phones when we talk so that "they" can't listen in on a cell phone. Who is "they," you wonder? I've never bothered to ask. I'm here to help Willow with whatever she needs, regardless of who her paranoia is directed at this week.

"Alright. But if you're going to walk down Main Street, make sure you're wearing your mask. These people are out in full force, and I don't need chaos to ensue after someone posts on social media that they spotted the elusive Iris Thornwick," Lucy tells me.

"Roger that," I say, my voice muffled by the rubber Halloween mask I've pulled back down to mask my identity. "Did you know this thing was modeled after William Shatner?"

"You're so full of shit," she says, motioning for me to exit the door while she shuts off the last row of lights, a gesture that I'm sure is second nature to her after the years she spent closing down the restaurant for us.

"I'm full of shit? Google it, bonehead."

We bicker for a few more minutes until we get to the edge of the parking lot. I take a right to head to Willow's apartment, while Lucy turns left, in the direction of our favorite dive bar.

"Don't take too long. I'm old, and I can't stay out as late as I used to," Lucy shouts before zipping up her fleece jacket to protect her neck from the early fall winds.

"Don't tell me what to do," I reply, and she smiles, shaking her head as she turns to leave.

I ignore the drunken revelers in the streets as I walk several blocks to the alley behind Willow's Nook, on the corner of Winston and Main. There's a rear entrance and a set of stairs that lead to her apartment above the shop. I passed by the front of the store before turning toward the alley; the lights were on, and a young girl was working behind the counter, helping the half dozen or so customers inside.

Like almost everyone in this town, October is Willow's busiest month of the year, but it's also the period of time she receives the most harassment and unwanted attention for her connection—both real and perceived—to my aunts' disappearances. She gladly pays a handful of local employees a few dollars above minimum wage to man the store for most of the month so she can stay upstairs. She tells me that she considers it money well spent.

The way tourists treat anyone who has a connection to my family is like a pack of wolves sniffing out their prey: If they realize we are *someone* in relation to the Thornwick case, they go rabid trying to get something from us. Whether it be a selfie or a video of us just trying to live our lives, or even a request to be on their god-awful podcasts, they won't stop until they have something tangible to brag to their online friends about.

It used to bother me a lot more than it does now, mostly because of a conversation I overheard my mother having with Willow a few years back. We'd dropped her off a to-go plate for Thanksgiving. She said one of the saddest days of her life was when the search party for her sisters was called off. The news crews left, the checkpoints for volunteers were broken down, and the streets were once again empty. Although she recognized that it probably wasn't healthy, she said when Westridge Cove became a tourist destination all those years later, it gave her a strange comfort. People cared about her sisters again. They may not be here to help her search, but they are just as passionate about getting answers. Every October, she's once again surrounded by people who are talking about Sarah, Bridget, and Maggie. The comfort makes it worth the chaos and it keeps their memories alive.

"Knock, knock," I shout while giving the door a few raps with the back of my hand.

A muffled grunt coming from the direction of the living room is my signal to come on in. Willow is sitting in her decades-old brown recliner with a folding tray in front of her. She has a stack of tarot cards next to a half-filled glass of milk on the tray and an old episode of *Matlock* playing on the newly purchased flat-screen TV that Mom and I bought her last Christmas. Several of the older shows she wanted to watch were available on streaming services, and once we showed her how easy it was to click a few buttons and pull up any episode she wanted, she was sold. The ancient, oversized beast of a TV was hauled away the next day, and a shiny new one from Walmart was delivered. She kept marveling about how amazing it is that all of these beloved shows are accessible for free, but that's only because she has no idea that Mom and I pay the monthly fee for her to have four different streaming services. One of the few expenses in life that are worth every penny.

"You know I do readings for you and your mother all the time," she says, rather than a normal greeting. She gives my mechanic jumpsuit a once-over, so I hold up the mask in my hand as an explanation. She shrugs.

"So you've told me," I reply, sitting on the loveseat a few feet from her. "You do readings for us, with or without our permission, and we're too tired to argue with you about it. I'm no expert, but aren't we supposed to be here when you pull the cards?"

"For the last two weeks, I keep getting the tower card when I'm reading you."

"Okay . . . care to tell me what that means?" I ask.

"I know how you kids can be when it comes to taking the word of an old spinster like me, so why don't you take that little computer of yours out and tell me what the World

Wide Web has to say about the meaning behind the tower card?"

My phone—that's what she refers to as my little computer. I pull it out of my shoulder bag and swipe to open the screen.

As I begin typing my search, she says, "Read the answer out loud, Iris."

When the results come up, I read the very first one.

"The tower tarot card signifies sudden, dramatic upheaval, destruction of false beliefs or structures, and forced liberation, often appearing as a shocking but necessary catalyst for profound change, revealing hidden truths and clearing the path for a more authentic new beginning."

I set my phone in my lap and look in her direction, waiting for her to elaborate.

"Well?" she asks.

"Well, what?"

"What the hell do you have cooking, Iris Thornwick? Something big is happening if I keep getting the tower card. I'm not stupid. You know about my intuitions, so I think it would be foolish of you to question them now."

"Willow, you called me all the way over here after a long shift, where I was getting my ass handed to me at the restaurant, so you could question me about the tarot card you keeping pulling on me while I'm not even here? How the hell would I know what it means?"

She looks down at the card in question, tilts her head as if deep in thought, and then looks back up at me.

"I saw on the news that they found a body by the museum today. I asked little Alexa as she was clocking in if she had heard anything about it. She told me the rumor is that it was Kellen DeYoung."

I nod.

"I heard that rumor, as well."

"You two were great friends as children. I'm sure you're upset to hear that he was killed, especially since they are saying it was in a fairly gruesome manner."

I wait a beat before responding.

"It's tragic. I hate to think that it's going to bring any stress onto our beloved Butthole Bucky, but my mom assured me that no publicity can be bad publicity in this town. I'm sure it'll be fine. Bucky and his darling wife will probably just add a reenactment of his death to the museum and charge extra to view it."

Willow has the same look my mom used to give me when I'd tell her I was staying over at a friend's house for a sleepover, but she had a sneaking suspicion that we'd be meeting up with boys down at the waterfront. Willow doesn't break eye contact with me when she responds.

"Be careful, Iris. Just be careful."

Chapter Eighteen

Lucy is outside the Alibi, leaning on the brick exterior and sipping a rum and Coke, when I make it to the bar after leaving Willow's. Thanks to Main Street's new designation as a social district, patrons can take their drinks to go during the month of October, but Lucy has been enjoying them outside long before it was legal.

"What are you doing out here, weirdo?" I ask.

"Intercepting your bitch ass," she responds.

"Oh God . . . Why?"

She takes another sip before motioning her head toward the door, right under the neon sign that at one time said The Alibi, but now has enough burned-out bulbs to read T e Al bi.

"I'm not gonna sugarcoat it, Iris. There are a lot of people you don't want to see in there, so I thought I'd give you the rundown, and you can decide if we should go in or just call it a night and get some gas station fried chicken and go back to the apartment."

I smirk. I can tell she'd actually love to get some chicken and get back into sweatpants, but she also loves drama. There's no denying it. Whoever is inside that bar could be a potential source of conflict, causing her immeasurable joy. She's a sick individual.

"Okay, lay it on me," I tell her, knowing she's chomping at the bit to list all the usual suspects.

"Let's start easy. Wally's at the bar. He's nursing a scotch and staring at the bar top, wondering if there's a killer on the loose in his little town or if Kellen's death was an isolated incident. Poor guy. Might be looking for some sex as a distraction."

She lifts an eyebrow and waits for my reaction, which is simply to roll my eyes.

"Go on."

"Next, we have Barrett Carter. He just lost his best friend, Kellen. They had such great memories together, including when they were eight years old and accused your teenage aunts of witchcraft, causing the entire town to want them dead. Boys will be boys, right?"

One of my favorite things about Lucy is that she also has a dark sense of humor. She knows she can joke about anything, including my dead aunts, and I'll laugh. It's a good quality to have in a friend.

"That it?"

I can see it in her eyes. She's preparing the best for last.

"Ann Haven is here. She just got done being questioned, I assume by Wally because you put the idea in his head, and is in the back corner telling everyone her dramatic tale of having a brush with death when Kellen's body was found on a parade float, sponsored by none other than her dumb boutique, Haven's Hats and Collectibles. That poor, poor woman. Who even wears hats anymore, anyways? How is she making money? She's probably money laundering."

I glance to my right and through the only window in the entire bar. I see everyone she just described—Wally, head hung in defeat; Barrett, on the opposite end of the bar, drinking away his sorrows; and in the back right corner, next to the bar, Ann Haven is in a booth with what appears to be a few PTO moms, telling them her story. She's gesturing wildly with her freshly manicured nails. As she takes a drink of her white wine, I envision storming in, grabbing the glass out of her hand, and breaking it over her head, which is topped with overgrown roots.

"Eh, fuck it. Let's go in," I say. I don't give her time to stop me before I open the thick wooden door and enter the bar. The sounds from inside spill out onto the street. A few heads turn as we walk in, but the Alibi is a bar for locals. I don't need my mask here. There isn't a face in the bar that I don't at least halfway recognize, and none of them have any interest in bothering me. It's a strange comfort during a month like October.

My eyes survey the room before I pick the least of the evils, Chief Wally Parker. Pulling out a barstool, I take a seat directly next to him, and he holds up his hand as if he's going to object before he sees it's me and comes to the same conclusion I did. I must be the least of the evils for him, as well. What an odd comfort.

"Glenlivet? I don't think I've seen anyone drink that since your dad at my grandma's memorial in 2013."

He holds up the glass of scotch at eye level, sloshing it around for a second before taking a healthy drink. "Judging by the layer of dust on the bottle, I'm not sure *anyone* has drunk it since 2013."

"Yeah," I reply, looking around at everyone else's drinks. "I fear this may be more of a PBR-and-shot-of-whatever's-on-sale kind of vibe."

He gives me the kind of smirk that acknowledges my quip, without giving me a full smile because he's hurting. I hate to be a source of stress for the man I've known my whole life, even though he's a pain in my ass. Hopefully he'll understand when this is all over that it needed to be done. He may not see it yet, but I'm doing him some favors.

"Can I buy you a drink?" he offers.

"I'll buy my own drink, but you can definitely do me the favor of getting Bailey's attention and ordering it for me. We got in an argument on Facebook during the last election, and she blocked me. I could be waving a hundred-dollar bill in the air, and she'll act like she's allergic to pouring me a fucking Coors Light."

This time, he cracks a little more than a smirk. He knows how I can be on social media. I don't log on often, but when I do, I sure have a bad habit of telling the idiots I went to school with exactly how I feel about their political opinions. My mom is worried, per usual, that my big mouth will affect our business at the café, so I told her I quit Facebook altogether. That seemed to satisfy her. It's going to be a tough dinner conversation when she finds out I'm still there. I just blocked her ass.

I turn my head to the right to face Lucy so Bailey won't realize the beer is for me. I nod toward Lucy's half-empty cocktail to see if she'd like me to have Wally order her another while he's at it, but she shakes her head.

"Nah, I've had a headache all day. Don't be mad, but I

think I might call it a night. I can barely keep my eyes open. You good?"

I smile and nod. She's been doing this a lot lately. I have no doubt she's tired, but I think tonight's early exit may be due to Lucy nudging me to spend more time with Wally. She's convinced we'll confess our feelings for each other eventually. Keep dreaming, lady.

Just as she's zipping her coat and saying her goodbyes, Wally slides a Coors Light in front of me with a shot glass filled with small lime wedges next to it.

"Did I ask for lime?"

"No, but you usually do," he says with a shrug. "The only person I know who drinks her Coors Light with a lime. It's kind of hard to forget."

Normally I'd make a joke about how he's paying too much attention to what I'm doing, but he looks so defeated, I simply thank him.

"Chin up, Wally. Nobody is going to blame you because you haven't made an arrest on a murder that happened hours ago. Give yourself some grace. Maybe you'll find out he was into some shady shit, and you'll discover a list of suspects who would have wanted him dead. Hell, you could just arrest Ann Haven and call it a day if you'd like. I don't think anyone would shed a tear about that bitch being behind bars."

I lean back on my barstool to shoot daggers at Ann, even though we're much too far away for her to hear our conversation. She most likely doesn't even know I'm here, but it still makes me feel good. Again, normally he would laugh at this. He despises Ann as much as I do for what she did to my aunts. He's just too distracted with Kellen's death to have a normal conversation.

He leans in closer to me, delivering his response in my

ear. This bar is so loud, I don't think anyone would be able to hear him anyway, but if I'm being honest, I don't mind him being so close. I can feel his warm, scotch-tinted breath on my ear and it sends a chill up my spine. I'll be the first to admit that my body tends to betray my brain when it comes to Wally Parker.

"That's just it, Iris. It hasn't been twenty-four hours since his death was announced, and we've already had three women come forward, accusing Kellen of unwanted sexual advances and stalking. I always knew he grew up to be an asshole, but I didn't know it was this bad. That opens up a whole new pool of suspects. Was it one of the women, one of their husbands, or a victim we don't even know about yet? How the hell am I going to figure out who killed Kellen while also handling tens of thousands of tourists who are coming to town this month? I'm just fucking overwhelmed. That's all."

I'll be honest; hearing that there may be a suspect pool this big makes my job a lot easier. Why would anyone suspect little ol' me? I decide to throw some added doubt to the situation, purely for my benefit.

"Or fuck, what about one of these obsessed fan boys who are on the message boards, convinced they were in love with my aunts? You know how it is on the internet these days. They blame the Carter and DeYoung boys for what happened. What if someone is trying to do a little vigilante justice because they're not quite right in the head?"

His phone, which is sitting face up on the bar top in front of him, illuminates with a message. He takes a second to read the screen, shakes his head, and then turns back to me.

"It's Bucky. He wants to call an emergency town meeting. Tomorrow morning at ten."

Chapter Nineteen

PRESENT DAY

There's no hiding the excitement in Butthole Bucky Lancaster's eyes as he discusses the untimely death of Kellen DeYoung. Where some may see tragedy, he sees dollar signs. A murder on the first day of tourist season, and the victim was a key player in the case that made this town famous? Bucky is practically salivating. If I didn't know any better, I'd think he killed Kellen himself to increase this month's bottom line.

"Ladies and gentlemen, I cannot stress to you the amount of added attention and business this tragedy is going to bring to our town. We need to be prepared."

He had to fight a giggle when he said the word tragedy, I swear it.

My attention goes to the shaking shoulders of my dear mother, who is trying unsuccessfully to control her sobs while she sits next to me.

"Mom," I say. "Really?"

"He was just a kid," she says, blowing her nose with

what appears to be a Taco Bell napkin. I can't imagine brown sandpaper is going to feel very good on her raw nostrils, but who am I to judge?

"He was like forty," I remind her.

"That's a kid to me, Iris. It's just so tragic."

I choose violence because I'll be damned if my sweet mother loses a minute of sleep over this jerk.

"I had a drink with Wally last night. He told me several women have come forward to give statements about Kellen's inappropriate behavior. Turns out he wasn't such a stand-up guy."

"Inappropriate behavior?" she asks, unable to believe that a *young boy* could be capable of it.

"Yes, Mom. He made several women very uncomfortable. He may have even stalked them. It's possible more will come forward. I wouldn't be surprised if one of their husbands found out and took justice into their own hands," I say, stealing Wally's theory.

She appears to consider this.

We return our attention to the mayor.

"It's important that we present a united message to the media: While this was a tragic event that resulted in the death of a beloved member of our community, there is no reason to believe that the public is at risk. The festivities shall proceed as planned," Bucky announces to the crowd. Again, with too much excitement in his voice, if you ask me.

His wife, Brighton, is sitting in the front row with the rest of the Junior League women. I'm sure they are debating which casserole to bring to Kellen's widow to display how compassionate they are, while also plotting when the best time to bring it over would be for maximum exposure to the local gossips, who will surely spread the word about their generosity. If they donate any money toward the funeral costs, it won't be until after they submit the details for a write up in the Westridge Gazette.

"How can the public not be at risk when Chief Parker doesn't seem to know who the hell did this?" shouts Gary, owner of the local meat market. While most of the eyes in the room travel to Wally Parker, a few inevitably look at me. They always do when Gary Bergland speaks because he seems to be the frontrunner when it comes to the rumors of who my biological father is. Mom has repeatedly insisted it's not true, and that Gary was simply a good friend of hers in high school. Sometimes I think I see a glimpse of my crooked smile, but it's probably just wishful thinking from a girl without a father.

Bucky motions for Wally to stand up and address the crowd.

"Everyone, I know how unsettling this is. A member of our community was tragically killed yesterday, and no arrests have been made. Although I can't comment much on an open investigation, I can confirm that we received several leads last night that I'm confident will push the investigation forward in the coming days. I can tell you that we do believe it was a targeted attack, and I see no need to cancel any scheduled events for the time being. Mayor Lancaster is right; this tragedy is expected to increase foot traffic this month, and we should all prepare for it. While there is no perceived threat to the general public, I'd advise you to stay vigilant as always. Any time a town the size of ours welcomes tourists in these numbers, things can get hairy really quick. We've called some officers over from Burntwood to help patrol the streets for the next few weeks. We're doing all we can to get some answers so we can put everyone's minds at ease. In the meantime, please do your best to run your businesses as usual."

You can actually hear the sighs of relief. This entire town is filled with money-hungry maniacs, I swear. A person in our own was killed, but thank *God* it won't affect business.

Lucy didn't show up for this morning's meeting, which is odd, but I decide to catch up with her later and give her hell for it. She's at work, but leaving to attend a town meeting has never been an issue before. When Gary Bergland raised his voice earlier, I could hear Lucy's inevitable joke about my *Meat Market Daddy* getting heated. A few years back, Gary was booked for a DUI after leaving a Super Bowl party while three sheets to the wind. His mugshot was making the rounds, as he had bloodshot eyes, a barbeque-stained shirt, and hair that looked like a young boy on Christmas morning. Lucy looked at the mugshot, then at me, and shrugged. "Honestly, I see the resemblance."

A few rows over, I notice Alexa, the employee Willow trusts the most to run the Nook while she hides upstairs all month. I smile when I see the notebook in her lap and her hand scribbling furiously to keep up with all the information being thrown out by Bucky. She wants to do a good job for Willow, and for that, I'm thankful. Mom says that Willow hasn't taken anyone under her wing since Aunt Sarah, and it's nice to see her finally trusting someone with her business.

"Does anyone have anything to add? If not, I'll consider this meeting adjourned, and we can all get back to preparing for the pandemonium," Bucky announces, with a little too much pep in his step.

"Yeah, I'd like to say something."

It's Barrett Carter—one of Kellen DeYoung's closest friends and one of the boys who were babysat by my aunts on that fateful night back in 1993. Every head in the room turns to face him. He looks like he hasn't slept in a week, despite the murder only happening yesterday. I recall his drunken head resting directly on the bar top at the Alibi last night as I was leaving.

"I think it's sick that everyone is talking about business while Kellen is lying in the morgue. Nobody seems to give a shit that we just lost one of the best men in this town."

It takes everything I have to resist spitting my coffee all over the back of Pastor Tom's head in front of me. Best men in this town? Give me a fucking break.

"I know the people of Westridge seem to think that the month of October is the only thing that matters, but I just lost my friend, and Chief Parker here seems to have no fucking idea who did it. Unlike our local law enforcement, I won't sleep until I find out who killed Kellen."

I bring my travel mug filled with steaming coffee to my lips to hide the smirk I'm fighting.

Barrett Carter can run his mouth all he wants about seeking justice, but he won't be around to see his friend receive any. I'll be making sure of that.

Chapter Twenty

OCTOBER 30TH, 1993

Rex Parker had planned to take the holiday weekend off. He was going to take Wally to Shopko over in Escanaba so he could pick out a costume. On Sunday, he'd watch the Packer game before he took Wally around the neighborhood for trick-or-treating. Instead, he's working on a Saturday, and that work includes knocking on the door of Nancy Thornwick's apartment so he can question her six-year-old daughter about her aunts' possible participation in witchcraft. He surely never imagined a situation like this when he took his oath to protect and serve.

"Chief Parker," Nancy said when she answered the door, more of a question than a greeting. Her hand instinctively traveled to her hair, insuring it wasn't a mess.

"Hi, Nancy. I sure am sorry to bother you on a Saturday, but I was hoping I could come in and ask you a few questions."

At twenty-four years old, Nancy Thornwick hadn't

broken many laws, but she did smoke a decent amount of homegrown pot from her friend Tommy, and that was enough to make her blood pressure rise at the sight of the chief of police at her door. She did a mental inventory of her apartment: Were there any joints lying around? Who would have ratted her out?

"You're not in any trouble. It's about your sisters."

Her hand flew to her chest.

"My sisters? Are they okay?"

"Yes, yes. They're fine. I just came from the house. I'm sure you've heard about the rumors regarding their behavior at the Carter home on Wednesday?"

Nancy furrowed her brows. She'd been working nonstop and hadn't heard any news about her sisters, or anyone else for that matter. Between dropping Iris off at school, cleaning houses all day, and picking her back up with time to cook dinner, watch the nightly news, and fight to keep her eyes open, there wasn't much time for idle gossip these days.

"Behavior?"

Rex couldn't believe Nancy hadn't heard the rumors by now. It's all anyone in town was talking about. He tried to have breakfast at Macy's Diner that morning but was hounded by nosey local retirees, with nothing better to do than gossip about three teenage girls and a ridiculous accusation by a gaggle of little boys. Well, and one eighteen-year-old, too, but he couldn't quite figure that one out yet. Ann Haven seemed to be hiding something when she gave her statement, but he had yet to figure out what it could be.

"Nancy, is your daughter home right now?"

"Iris? She's in her room watching Saturday morning cartoons. Why?"

"Do you mind if we sit down for a minute?"

Nancy led him to her small living area, where he took a seat on the edge of the couch, and she followed suit on the matching loveseat.

He'd been dealing with these accusations for a couple of days now, but it never ceased to feel ridiculous saying them out loud.

"I'm sorry to be the one to tell you this, but the Carter and DeYoung boys are reporting that your sisters were performing some sort of satanic rituals on Wednesday night. I'm here to talk to Iris and see if she saw anything strange while she was in their care. Has she said anything about the girls casting spells? The accusations are a little hazy."

Rex braced for Nancy's reaction, but was met with silence and a wide-eyed stare. Then, she threw her head back and began to laugh so aggressively that tears formed at the corners of her eyes.

"I've heard of some good Devil's Night pranks, but this one takes the cake. Let me guess—Sarah was the ringleader, and she learned the spells from Willow Nora? Oh wait, did Maggie fly home on a broom while Bridget rode her bike? Maybe they listened to that Judas Priest album backwards and were manipulated by the devil. Please, go on. Don't let your officers think you failed while trying to pull one over on me. Who put you up to this, anyway?" She laughed for a few more seconds and took a drink from her can of Diet Pepsi, sitting on the coffee table between them. She only recently started drinking it again after a syringe-in-the-can hoax that caused nationwide panic. "I needed a laugh today."

Nancy leaned back on the couch, waiting for Rex to slap his leg and say, "Well, damn it. I guess I'll try again next year," but that never came. The look of absolute sincerity in his eyes nearly broke her.

"Nancy, I understand how shocking this may seem, but half of this town believes the rumors and are demanding I do something about it. People will do anything to protect their children; I know you can sympathize with that."

She had to wait for a second, somehow still foolishly waiting for him to admit it was a joke, before responding.

"Chief Parker, if you'd like a statement from me, you can write this down: My three little sisters are the sweetest, smartest, most special kids you'd ever be lucky enough to know. And I call them kids because that's exactly what they are. I can't believe I need to say this out loud, but no, I don't believe any of them are experienced in casting spells, doing seances, or whatever the hell you're accusing them of. In fact, I was there that night, twice—once to drop Iris off and then again to pick her up when my plans got changed. Nothing strange was happening at all, and I'm certain my daughter would agree with that, should you insist on interrogating a six-year-old."

Rex held his hands up in defense.

"Nancy, I'm not here to interrogate anyone. I just want to either speak with Iris or sit here while you ask her a few questions, so I can mark this off my list and move on. I've known your family longer than you've been alive, and between you and me, this is all a bit ridiculous. However, I am the chief of police, and it's my job to thoroughly investigate any accusations made in this town."

Rex flinched as Nancy loudly yelled for Iris to come into the room. He was never great at reading women, but he knew he had pissed this one off. The sweet little girl came padding into the living room, still wearing her pink unicorn pajamas and holding a Barbie doll in her left hand.

"Iris, honey, you remember Chief Parker? He's a friend of Grandma and Grandpa's, and he's also Wally's dad."

Iris' thumb traveled to her mouth, a habit that was happening more infrequently these days, but still reared its head when she was uncomfortable. She looked over Rex and nodded.

"We were just sitting here talking about last week when you got to go over to the Carters' house and hang out with your aunts. Do you remember that?" Nancy asked, careful not to nod or lead her daughter in any way. As annoyed as she was at the situation, she'd also watched enough police procedural shows to know that the answers needed to come directly from Iris without outside influence.

"Yes, we had pizza, and Wally licked his finger and put it in my ear, and I told him that is gross."

"He saw it on a cartoon," Rex replied, feeling the need to explain his son's behavior to Nancy. "I'm hoping he grows out of it."

Nancy ignored Rex and kept her attention on Iris.

"Okay, sweetie, tell me what else you guys did."

Iris looked up to the ceiling and tapped her little index finger on her chin. It would be adorable, if Nancy wasn't so disturbed about the line of questioning that she was forced to put her daughter through.

"Oh, we watched a movie! Three witches. They were so scary. And a man was in the graveyard, and he came back to life, and there was a cat that could talk. Also, they flew through the air."

Nancy shot a look at Rex.

Rex hung his head. He wanted this investigation to be over as much as anyone else.

"Well, that sounds scary. And then what did you guys do?" he asked the little girl.

She again considered the question.

"I got really sleepy, and Aunt Maggie carried me into a

bedroom, but she left the door open because I was too scared to be in the dark. And then I was even more sleepy, and my mommy came and got me and put me in the car. Aunt Maggie promised me Mickey Mouse pancakes, but Mommy said we got too much sleep and didn't have time to make them before school."

That's the thing about kids: They may not remember their homework, but they'll remember every damn thing you promised them until the moment you deliver.

"That's all I needed to know, sweetie. You can go ahead and finish watching your cartoons," Nancy told her. Iris clapped her hands together before sprinting back into her room to finish *Taz-Mania*.

"Why is it that you needed a babysitter in the first place?" Rex asked as he stood to leave.

"I was going to a concert. The original plan was for my sisters to take Iris back to my parents for the night, and I'd pick her up in the morning, but my plans changed, so I ended up showing up at the Carters' to take her home."

He couldn't help but notice that she seemed flustered by the question.

"And who were you going to the concert with?"

"A guy from work."

Rex wasn't aware of any guys who cleaned houses with Nancy.

"And why the change of plans?"

"He wasn't feeling well, and the roads were a little slick. We just decided to call it a night and gave the tickets to some friends."

Rex had known Nancy Thornwick since the day she was born. Even if he didn't do this for a living, he'd have spotted that lie from a mile away.

Chapter Twenty-One

PRESENT DAY

When I arrive at the café, Mom is having a pre-shift meeting with the servers and hosts before the lunch rush. She's wearing a black nylon robe and is holding a Ghostface mask in her hand. *Scream* is always the most low-effort costume for both of us and usually doesn't make the rotation until the end of the month, when we are out of ideas. Kellen's death must be getting to her more than I realized.

"Every table leaves happy; that's our motto. If there's an issue, grab me or Iris. These customers have come from all over the country, and they could have chosen any restaurant in town, but they chose us. Let's not forget that. Even if these people can be a little difficult, they are still the ones paying our bills. The lunch special today is the cod sandwich with hand-cut fries. Is everyone on the same page on what to say if you're asked about Iris or me?"

The employees respond in near unison, as we've been over this more times than I could count: "Nancy and Iris

Thornwick always spend the month of October in Florida with a relative." Do we have any relatives in Florida? No, we don't. Somehow, the lie seems to work every year. They believe it and quit looking at everyone's Halloween costume, wondering if it might be a Thornwick.

Mom ends the meeting with the same phrase she's been using for years: "Let's feed these people, send them home happy, and make some money. I appreciate all of you." A lot of business owners and managers govern with fear; Mom earns their respect through kindness and hard work. During a long shift, you won't find anyone working like Nancy Thornwick, and luckily, she's instilled that same work ethic in me. She's the reason this café is so successful; I'm just lucky to be following in her footsteps.

I stopped at home to throw my costume on after the town hall meeting, and I also chose a low-effort option for today's look—a pumpkin. With brown tights, an orange pullover, and brown felt pieces glued on the front to complete the jack-o-lantern look, it's a dependable disguise I've been using for at least five years. My hair is tied into a high bun, and I have a simple brown mask that mimics the little stump that comes from the top of the pumpkin.

The day goes exactly as I'd envisioned on my walk to work—absolute yet controlled chaos. The volume never let up; we had a line out the door for the entirety of the shift. I lost count of how many of our employees suffered minor or major mental breakdowns during the rush, but I suspect it was all of them. I keep a pack of Oreos in the manager's office, specifically for this reason, and the package was empty by two that afternoon.

One of the big differences between tourists and locals is that if a local has an issue with the food or service, they'll mention it to me or my mom. When a tourist is disappointed with their experience, they feel the need to tell the world. Their grubby little fingers are logged on to Yelp before the check hits the table. Our job is, first, to minimize the chances our guests will have a negative experience and, second, to fix any issues immediately so they don't feel the need to tell the world not to eat at Thornwick Café. Mom took over the Yelp account because I was "blurring the lines of what's acceptable to say to a customer" while responding to one-star reviews. Whatever that means.

The Westridge Country Club women, who also happen to be the same women who are on the Junior League board of directors, come in around 2:30 and Mom has the nerve to reserve them a table in the corner. We don't take reservations, and we damn sure don't cater to the wives of the richest assholes in town, yet Mom continues to bend the knee whenever they come calling.

We assign Nikki to the table because, despite hating them as much as I do, she's fantastic with that kind of crowd. She plays the single-mother-who-just-can't-catch-a-break persona with ease, and it usually bodes well for her tips. Reluctantly, I check on the women just as they are finishing their lunches.

"Iris!"

I shake my head rapidly at Brighton Lancaster, but the damage may have already been done. She said my name loud enough for half the restaurant to hear. I can sense the whispers and heads turning my way.

"Yes, Iris is in Florida until November," I respond, nodding my head slowly, and desperately begging for these self-centered, affluent bitches to remember the one thing we talk about every single September before the chaos begins. Even Butthole Bucky remembers to mention it to the locals: Never, ever acknowledge that the Thornwicks or Willow

Nora are anywhere in Westridge Cove during tourist month. It will create a panicked mob of looky-loos who want a picture or a statement from us. Mom, Willow, and I may be the only three non-money crazed lunatics around here, because most people would weep when they saw the dollar amounts we've turned down for interviews. We've never done one, and we don't plan to anytime soon. I'm not sure why they want to interview me anyway; I was only six and have very few memories of my aunts at all, let alone from the week of their disappearances.

Sorry, Brighton mouths to me, but she's not sorry. She's a horrible person. Carol Carter and Bev Friarson practically roll their eyes at the situation, as if I'm overreacting. The hushed voices coming from the booths surrounding us tell me that I'm not exaggerating a damn thing. They might not be sure it's me, but they are suspicious enough to be staring and discussing the possibility. Through gritted teeth, I thank the women for their business and head to the kitchen to pull my mask off and take a breather. One day, maybe Mom and I *will* spend this godawful month at the beach, once we have someone trustworthy enough to run this place in our absence. If I'm being honest, I don't see that happening anytime soon.

"You good, Iris?"

It's Luis, one of my favorite cooks. He's been with us for years.

"Yeah, just got a little overwhelmed. I'll be okay."

"Want me to cut someone?" he asks, momentarily lifting his knife from the onion he's slicing.

I consider it.

"Nah, but I'll let you know if I change my mind."

"Fair," he says with a wink.

I hear a popping noise coming from behind me, and I

whip around to see Mom punching in one of the cardboard boxes that holds the fountain pop syrup, so she can access the spout and hook it to the machine. They are technically called B.I.B.s, or Bag-in-Boxes, and after decades of supplying them to nearly every restaurant in existence, you'd think they'd come up with a better packaging system that doesn't give us all bloody knuckles trying to punch them open.

"Today is supposed to be your short day, sweetie," Mom tells me, wiping her hands off on the black robe of her costume. "Why don't you get out of here?"

We are all working six- and seven-day work weeks this month, but we try to give each other a "short day" once a week, which requires us to work just one of the rushes and then we can head home. Normally, I'd refuse and tell her I have enough stamina for the dinner rush, but I'm feeling a little run down today and could sure use the rest.

"Let me just inventory the freezer before I leave so Luis doesn't have to do it. I know he's been working a lot of hours."

"You're not touching my freezer, Mami; I have it orga-nized just the way I like. Go home," Luis yells from his prep station. Mom smiles.

"Alright, I'll leave. But I'll have my cell phone on, so just call or text if you need me to come back. I'm going to take a hot bath and stare at the wall for a while."

"The official pastime of restaurant employees during peak season," Mom says, patting me on the back. "Now, get out of here. I'll see you in the morning."

She doesn't have to tell me again; I pull my mask back over my face, grab my bag and keys, and head out the back door of the restaurant. I'm hoping Lucy is at the apartment so we can gossip about what a bitch Brighton Lancaster is before I pour my bath.

Although I'm trying my darndest to quit, I remember there's a half-filled vape in my bag, and am in desperate need of the jolt of happiness I get from taking a hit. I reach down into the bottom of the bag next to my wallet and ChapStick, and my fingers detect the familiar shape. I pull my mask up, and I'm taking a quick inhale when I hear the words.

"It's her! It's Iris Thornwick! It's fucking her!"

Well, shit.

I pull my mask back down, but it's too late. These Halloween-loving heathens have discovered what they came to Westridge Cove to see—a Thornwick.

"Iris, we love you!" one of them yells as I speed up my pace.

Within a block, I glance back to see the crowd has grown, and there are now nearly a dozen people following me, like a scene from the *Walking Dead*.

"Iris, can we get a selfie?"

"Iris, will you be on my podcast?"

"Iris! I communicated with your aunts from the other side! They have a message for you!"

Despite the dropping temperatures, I'm now breaking out in a sweat. My brown tights are beginning to rub the skin on my thighs raw from walking so fast, and the waistband is cutting into my lower abdomen. I just need to make it home. Why the hell did I think it was safe to pull up my mask in the middle of broad daylight? This is all my fault. I glance back once more. Several more have joined the group, and wouldn't you know it—one of them even has *my* face on his shirt. I don't stay turned around long enough to read the whole thing, but I believe I saw the words "the Next Generation of Witch." If they only knew.

I pick up the pace even more when I reach the corner where I need to take a right to make it the final two blocks to my and Lucy's apartment. As soon as I make the turn, the side door of a brick building flies open, and an arm reaches out, grabbing me around the waist and pulling me into the dark landing of a stairwell, the door slamming behind me. I can hear shouts outside when the mob turns the corner and realizes I'm gone. "Where did she go?" "Which way did she turn?"

I'm pressed up against the wall, my heart pounding so rapidly I think I may have a coronary event, when my eyes adjust enough to see who pulled me into the building.

"Wally?" I whisper, my breaths ragged.

He holds an index finger to his lips as we hear several of the voices nearing the door, just inches from where we stand. His right arm is still wrapped around me, hand pressed firmly on my lower back, protecting me from the wall he pushed me against when he pulled me inside.

"I was upstairs doing a welfare check when I saw commotion outside. I ran downstairs as quickly as I could," he whispers, leaning so far forward that our foreheads are nearly touching.

The adrenaline running through my system is clouding my thoughts. All I can focus on is his scent—fresh evergreen mixed with the hand sanitizer he carries everywhere.

I'm not sure why I do it, but I lift my mask and raise my gaze to meet his. I don't need to make the choice because he makes it for me. He leans in and his lips touch mine. Soft, sweet, and lingering. He takes his time before pulling away.

"I've wanted to kiss you for as long as I can remember," he whispers.

There's a million reasons why I shouldn't, but must admit, I feel the same way.

Chapter Twenty-Two

PRESENT DAY

"Iris, you've killed two people with plans to kill more, and you decided that maybe it would be a good idea to hook up with the chief of fucking police in a fucking stairwell? Be so for real right now—what the hell are you thinking?"

So, Lucy isn't thrilled with what went down. I could have kept this one to myself, but I don't keep secrets from her. I've tried, but she's a master at sniffing it out when I'm hiding something. She's like a human lie detector test with a zero-percent fail rate.

"I mean, I didn't *plan* for it to happen," I tell her, plunging a corkscrew into a bottle of wine from our kitchen counter. "I was running for my life, Lucy. My adrenaline must have clouded my judgement."

She cocks her head dramatically, as if she couldn't imagine something more exhausting than dealing with me in this moment.

"Running for your life, or running from a gaggle of twenty-somethings wanting a selfie?"

"How was I to know their intentions? All I know is that there was a mob of people chasing me, and Wally saved me, and the next thing I know, we were making out. I don't see why you're so upset about this; you're always the one making comments about how we need to hook up. In fact, you've been pushing the issue for at least twenty years. I figured you'd be overjoyed."

She leans forward on the counter between us and shakes her head.

"Iris, you aren't getting it. I don't agree with what you're doing with these killings, but I'm not stopping you because maybe a part of me does agree that they need to pay for what they did. I secretly hope you and Wally end up together some day. I just don't think you need to initiate a relationship with him in the middle of your homicidal rage tour. It will only bring unnecessary stress to the both of us. What am I going to do if you get caught? I sit here while you plot out your crimes— I'm no expert, but I believe that makes me an accessory. Especially when you killed the Burntwood Burglar; I was literally there. He wasn't even supposed to be part of the plan. You were only supposed to kill the guys who were there that night."

"And I told you that I needed to kill someone to prove to myself that I could do it before I planned Kellen's death. Who better to practice on than the guy who was terrorizing women for months?"

I finish a heavy pour into my glass and hold the bottle toward her, but she shakes her head, declining my offer. When we decided to take out the Burntwood guy, it didn't take much convincing on my end to get her to go along with it—he was a horrible man. Now she seems to be doubting the entire plan. She's getting cold feet, but I sure as hell am not.

"I'm not saying he didn't deserve to die. If I'm being honest, it kind of felt good to watch. But if you're going to pull off the other murders, you need to cut out the distractions. Wally Parker is a distraction. He's also the man who could get you locked up for life if he finds out. Please just . . . be careful. You're my best friend, Iris; you're like a sister to me. This should show you that I'd do anything for you, but if you want to get away with this, you've got to be more careful. There's literally an urban legend that you kill men, and now you're doing it for real."

"I mean, it's kind of like hiding in plain sight or whatever, right? If all these tourists have their made-up theories about how all the Thornwick women are murderous man haters, who would actually think it's true? It's exactly what you said—an urban legend. Nobody on that police force would suspect that I'm killing these men after I've lived alongside them my entire life. Why now, over thirty years later? There would be no logical reason for it."

She changes her mind and reaches into the cupboard for a wine glass, pouring herself enough to calm her nerves.

"You're doing the right thing, Iris. I know you are. It doesn't mean that I'm not scared shitless about it."

Chapter Twenty-Three

OCTOBER 30TH, 1993

One more harassing phone call and Sheila Thornwick was going to drive down to the telephone company and change their number. They'd had the landline since she and Peter got married, and it broke her heart to think they'd have to give it up just to put an end to the madness. It was Halloween weekend. Didn't these people have anything better to do than harass three teenage girls?

Again, the phone rang. Maggie, who rarely lost her cool, stomped across the linoleum to answer it while the rest of the family sat in various spots in the kitchen. Peter would be home from his shift soon, and Sheila didn't know where to begin to fill him in on the events of the last two days.

"Yes?" she answered with an irritated tone, a far departure from her usual, "Thornwick residence, this is Maggie!"

"What in the hell have you three gotten yourselves into?"

Maggie exhaled. Hearing her sister's voice was like

having a big drink of water after being stranded in the desert all day.

"Nancy," she said, causing every head in the kitchen to turn her way. "It's so bad."

"Rex Parker just left. What in the hell is this all about? You idiots were fine when I picked up Iris."

"We don't know, Nance. We played some games; it was just totally normal stuff. We have no idea where the hell this all came from. They are saying that Ann Haven told Chief Parker that we did some sort of witchcraft with the kids. It's all so crazy. Why would she do that?"

Sarah got up and pulled the receiver out of Maggie's hands. Maggie didn't have the energy to throw a fit; she simply sank into one of the barstools at the counter next to the phone and hung her head.

"Nancy, what the hell are we going to do? People have been calling the house all day, saying we deserve to be hung like the witches in Salem. They egged the house. They called us so many names at school, we had to leave. It's so fucked up," Sarah told her. "It's like this whole town has turned into an angry mob that doesn't care about knowing what actually happened."

"Language," Sheila said, but there was such little energy behind the warning, she decided as soon as the word left her lips that she'd no longer care what kind of language her girls used. They were being accused of so much worse, who should care about a few swear words during a time like this.

The doorbell rang, and it may have well been gunshots firing in the night, the way it made all their hearts stop.

"I'll handle it. You girls stay in the kitchen," Sheila instructed them.

She slowed her pace when she detected several figures on her front porch, their features blurred by the frosted glass of the side light next to her front door. It appeared to be three people waiting for her, but she couldn't be sure that there weren't more, possibly standing out of view. Hesitantly, she pulled the door open to reveal three older women from the neighborhood.

"Hello, Sheila," one of them said while all three sets of eyes traveled up and down to take in her appearance. Between her uncombed hair, fuzzy slippers, and the bathrobe she threw back on over her clothes, she wasn't exactly the picture of a put-together housewife.

Sheila clocked their disapproving facial expressions and pulled the belt on her robe a little tighter around her waist.

"How can I help you ladies?" she asked, without a hint of kindness in her voice. She was done being kind.

"We're here on behalf of the Westridge Women's Bible Study group at St. Francis Church. We thought you could use a little guidance."

"Guidance?" she asked. If there were ever a picture of someone on the verge of blowing their lid, it would have resembled Sheila Thornwick preparing to hear the answer to this question.

The women looked to each other before the one on the right, who Sheila believes is also the church treasurer from the limited times she's attended mass, spoke up first.

"Sheila, God is good all the time, and he loves all his children. We all have sinned and fallen short of the glory of God. It is not too late for your children to repent, to denounce the name of Satan and rid their hearts and their minds of his evil influence."

The other two clutched the sterling silver crosses around their necks as the woman spoke, as if the mere mention of Satan would somehow seep into their pores and take over their minds.

"What did you say your name was?" Sheila asked, dropping her arms from holding the robe's belt around her waist.

"Betty Nichols, dear."

"And Betty, I'm assuming with a town this small that you've seen my daughters around . . . probably since they were babies?"

The woman nodded hesitantly, unsure where this was going.

"And what behavior have you seen from my sweet girls, I mean actually seen with your own eyes, that would lead you to believe these horrible rumors that they are worshipping Satan?"

"Well, that middle one has been wearing sneakers and black clothing all semester long. I know your oldest has quite the taste in music and spends a lot of time with the widow Nora. I would presume the youngest was just going along with her older sisters."

Sheila gives her a tight smile.

"I haven't done much bible studying lately, but I believe it was John 7:24 that mentions not judging by appearances?"

"We didn't come here to upset you, dear; we just came to let you know that we are praying for your girls and wondered if we could be of any help. We would be happy to come inside and pray over them," the third woman said.

"If you'd like to help me, what you can do is drag your sorry, judgmental, pious asses back here once my daughters are cleared of all wrongdoing and you find out that this was all a ridiculous hoax, and you can stand on this very porch and tell me how sorry you are for believing such nonsense about my sweet daughters. And then I'll do the same thing I'm going to do now—shut this damn door in your face. I haven't been to church in months, and somehow, I'm living a life that Christ would be proud of more than you nosey bitches ever could. Now kindly, piss off."

And with that, Sheila slammed the door in the faces of the women from church, and she wasn't sure anything she'd done in her fifty years on this earth had ever felt so good.

Sarah, who was giving Nancy a play-by-play over the phone, was the only daughter with a mouth that wasn't hanging wide open when Sheila returned to the kitchen.

"Holy shit," Nancy said on the other end of the phone. "I've never heard Mom talk like that. Okay, I'll be over in the morning, and we can figure out what the hell we're going to do about all of this. Try to stay out of trouble tonight, will you?"

Chapter Twenty-Four

PRESENT DAY

After being chased by a hungry mob and subsequently pulled into a dark stairwell to make out with a man I've known my entire life, the rest of the week seemed pretty uneventful.

Mom and I have continued to elude detection in our Halloween costumes, and although fatigued, our employees have fallen into the routine required to handle the elevated level of business. We're always slammed in October; it's just never been quite at this level before.

Today is my day off, and I use that term lightly because it only means that I'm at the restaurant at seven in the morning to help with inventory and product orders and can head back home after I finish and post the employee schedule. I smile when I see that one of our newer employees requested two days off this month, bless her heart. I've only posted No Time Off Requests in October signs on every square inch of the fucking restaurant.

I'm finishing the last day of the schedule when my

phone vibrates. My heart skips a beat when I see the name on the screen: Wally. His contact picture is Dewey, the cop played by David Arquette in the *Scream* movies, and it makes me smile each time it pops up on my phone. He'd be annoyed to see the picture assigned to his name, but a small-town cop who has little to no experience investigating murder is the perfect comparison.

Wally has been in the café a few times since our little rendezvous, but we've yet to have a private conversation. I did throw an extra mint in with his check last Friday as a token of my affection, but I'm not sure he got the message.

"Are you still taking today off?" he asks.

"Are you stalking my schedule?" I reply.

Three little dots pop up and disappear several times before his reply is delivered.

"Maybe."

"What's it to you?" I ask, leaning back in my office chair. I don't even notice that I'm smiling until my cook, Luis, pops his head in the office and asks who's got me in such a good mood.

"Your dad," I respond. "We went out last week and now he won't stop texting me."

"My dad's dead, Iris."

"My bad," I say, and he gives me a wicked grin.

"Just kidding. He lives in Mexico; I just wanted you to feel bad."

I gasp. "Well done, Luis. You're learning the game. I'm proud."

He shakes his head and returns his attention to the clipboard he's holding. I look down to see that Wally responded immediately to my question, and I left him hanging.

"Can I buy you a cup of coffee somewhere other than the café so we can chat for a minute?"

"Sure," I type back. "I'll meet you at Delightful Donuts in fifteen."

I choose the place and time so that this man doesn't get the impression that he's in control of anything. I've got to keep him on his toes.

Fifteen minutes later, he's the one keeping me on *my* toes when I walk into the donut shop and see that he's already seated, and he's taken the liberty of ordering for me.

"Awfully bold of you to assume you know what I was going to order," I tell him as I pull my jacket off and throw it into the booth before I take a seat.

"Awfully bold of you to assume that Larry wouldn't tell me that you've been ordering a vanilla cinnamon latte and Bavarian crème donut every week for the last decade."

I shoot a glance over at Larry, one half of the couple who has owned Delightful Donuts since 1988, and he simply shrugs and returns to wiping the counter over the display case. The betrayal.

"You guys don't know; I could have been in the mood for something new," I say, taking a bite of my sugary, crème-filled piece of heaven. My eyes involuntarily roll back in my head—it's even more delicious than the one I ordered last week on my way to work. I don't know how Larry does it, and he won't give me the recipe.

"Judging by your facial expressions, I don't think you have any interest in ordering a different donut, Iris."

There's something about the way he says my name—a voice I've listened to my entire life suddenly sounds so sweet. His sideways smirk, slight stubble even though it's only eight in the morning, the definition in his jaw. Have I always been in love with this man? Has Lucy been right this entire time? Whenever I'd hear stories of people falling in love after being friends for years, I was always a little repulsed by the idea of inexplicably becoming attracted to someone I'd known that long. I just didn't think it was possible. Now, here I sit, getting sick to my stomach with nerves over a man who I saw naked when we were only in diapers.

"So, why did you want to see me?" I ask, wiping sugar from the edge of my mouth.

"I received a courtesy call this morning from WKTV. They're airing an interview with Ann Haven tonight and wanted to get a statement from my dad. I let them know that Dad isn't in any condition to be giving a statement, but I asked her if she'd give me a heads up on the content of the interview. Iris, they said Ann is going to recant her confession to police. She's going to admit that your aunts weren't involved in anything at all with us kids."

The news hits me like a punch right to the middle of the chest, stealing the air from my lungs. Ann's police interview with Rex Parker, Wally's dad, was widely seen as the only credible accusations against my aunts. The rest of the interviews were with six- and eight-year-old boys and could have been chalked up to active imaginations after watching a movie about witches. Ann's words brought validity to the claims. Her statement changed everything. My Mom and my grandparents tried to meet with her for years to understand why she did it. Why would she lie about three sisters who had been great friends to her for years? She'd refused all meetings and rarely showed her face in public until after my grandparents had passed away. My mom isn't a violent person, but her little hands ball up in fists whenever we see Ann in public.

"Can you arrest her?"

"Not for this. The statute of limitations would prevent any sort of criminal charges."

"Why would she choose now to come forward?"

He shakes his head while considering the question.

"I'm not sure, but I'd guess it has something to do with Kellen's death. Maybe she's trying to come clean and change the public's perception of her. If she makes a sincere public apology, maybe she thinks there won't be as much of a target on her back."

"So she's doing it to save her own ass; imagine that. Did they tell you what she plans to say, as far as her reasons for accusing my aunts of these things?"

"No," he says, defeat in his eyes. "I tried to get the producer to give me anything, but she was pretty tight-lipped about it."

I know I'll watch the interview, especially because I'm off tonight, but the thought of seeing her smug face on the screen, most likely spewing more lies, just infuriates me.

"Wally, tell me, did my aunts ever do anything to make you uncomfortable? Did they do anything to make you feel like they were capable of the things they were accused of?"

He places a hand over mine in the center of the table, and I instinctively look over to make sure Larry isn't watching. I'm not sure why I care; it's not like we're fifteen years old anymore.

"Iris, I was just shy of seven years old when they disappeared, so I don't have a lot of clear memories of them. What I can promise you is that I only remember the laughs, the games, the way I looked forward to the nights that Dad told me the sisters would be babysitting me. That may have just been because I knew you'd be there, but I don't remember ever being uncomfortable or afraid of them. Not even close."

"Me neither," I say, gently squeezing his hand before pulling it away and back into my lap. "You know, I've read up a lot on the whole satanic panic thing as an adult. In almost every documented case, it was just normal kids or adults becoming victims of these mobs of angry parents or neighbors who hated them because they viewed them as being different. Have you read up on the West Memphis Three case? It's enough to make you sick. Those boys were persecuted because of the way they looked and the books they read. I can't help but think that this town believed what they were hearing about my aunts because Sarah spent so much time with Willow Nora. It just made the rumors a little easier to believe."

"Yeah, I watched a documentary on those West Memphis boys," he tells me. "I think a lot of people find it easier to hate the things they don't understand. Because of that small town's obsession with proving those three killed the little boys, they neglected to follow a lot of other leads. Leads that could have resulted in catching the real killer. Or killers. Your aunts' case is a little different because I just don't believe there was even a crime committed. I think Kellen, Barrett, Logan, and Jack were just confused little kids who had active imaginations. I just can't figure out why Ann Haven went along with it. She could have been the one person to shut that shit down immediately. She was there all night with you guys."

"Well, I guess we'll find out tonight on the nightly news, now, won't we?" I say, still not believing that Ann is going on live TV to discuss this case for the first time. You'd think she'd have the decency to say what she needed to say to our faces. She doesn't need a camera for that. She knows where we live.

"Should we watch it together?" Wally asks, raising an eyebrow. "You know, to compare notes."

"Are you asking me on a date to watch the local news, Wally Parker?"

"I suppose I am," he says, the right side of his mouth twitching slightly as his lips curl into a smile. "Want to come to my place around five? I'll whip up something for us to eat before the interview airs at six."

Eating a homecooked meal instead of the café fries I've been stealing on the go because I'm too busy sounds like a dream. Hanging out at Wally's so I don't have to hear Lucy's thoughts on my budding relationship with the chief of police sounds even better.

Chapter Twenty-Five

PRESENT DAY

I decide to drive to Wally's rather than walk so that I don't have to wear a mask. My pores are clogged from all the sweating, and I just did an at-home mud mask treatment in a desperate attempt to do some damage control. I do, however, pull the hood of my jacket up and slide on a pair of oversized sunglasses before I put the car in drive. I can't risk some maniac recognizing me and trying to take a picture through my windshield. I only deal with this one month out of the year; I'm not sure how celebrities do this every day. It's exhausting, and I feel like I'm always on edge.

Luckily, the Westridge Cove Carnival kicks off tonight, so the crowds have mostly migrated away from Main Street and over to Cameron Park, on the edge of the Boney Hills Forest. At this time in October, the three-acre lot is filled with a Ferris wheel, carnival games, a haunted house, and every food you could possibly think to fry and put on a stick.

The place will be packed until it closes on the twenty-fifth, and Kayla's Haunted Korn Maze opens on the opposite side of town and runs past Halloween night. One thing that Butthole Bucky got right: Nobody will be bored in Westridge during the month of October. He may be a rich, miserable bastard, but he's made sure there's something for everyone in this town.

I pull into Wally's driveway, and it slows my heart rate like I'm coming home. He lives in the house he grew up in—a navy-blue craftsman with two hanging swings on the oversized white porch. He moved back in years ago to take care of Rex when his health started to decline. After his dad had an unfortunate incident last year and was moved into the assisted living home, Wally has been here on his own.

I spent a lot of time here as a kid, usually begging Wally and his friends to let me play with them and picking up worms with my bare hands to prove to them that I was worthy of being the only girl in the group. I glance at the old oak tree at the edge of the property and remember the day the boys dared me to climb it, which was a successful dare until I hopped down and skinned both knees.

Until Lucy moved here in the third grade, I was always the only girl in the group. I'd never met anyone like her. I'd always felt so alone around girls my age, and finally I had met someone just like me. She loved getting dirty, cussing, and playing rough. Instantly, she was one of us. I'm not sure when she decided that Wally and I should be a thing, but she's been pushing the issue for as long as I can remember. I thought she was going to die of happiness when I agreed to go to the Homecoming dance with him. She was none too thrilled when the relationship fizzled out soon after.

I guess this is our second chance, and it couldn't come at a worse time. I'm on a vendetta tour of violence, and Lucy is right: I'm being reckless by spending my free time with the man who could arrest me for my crimes.

I jog up the steps and Wally opens the front door to greet me. I'm equal parts happy to see his face while also flustered because I didn't have time to mentally prepare what I'd say.

"Hi," he says.

"Hi," I reply, and neither of us moves. There's something in the air, a realization that we're done fighting this. It's finally happening. No more quips, insults, or one-upping each other. We no longer need to fear being the first one to admit their feelings because we've somehow caved at the same time. It's so satisfying.

He's changed out of his uniform and into a dark gray henley, faded jeans, and fresh-from-the-shower wet hair. *Swoon.*

"Come on in. I picked up some steaks from your daddy," he says with a wink, and I'm so relieved that he's still joking with me like we have for years, I end up laughing entirely too loud in response.

"I told you, Mom swears there's no truth to it," I reply as he moves aside and motions for me to come in.

"I was there when his mugshot was taken. I sent it to Lucy and we laughed so hard we couldn't breathe. There's an undeniable resemblance, Iris."

"Fuck you," I say with a smirk. "So, steaks, huh? Since when do you know how to cook a steak?"

He leads me into the kitchen, where he has a small pub-style table set for two. There's a candle lit in the middle of the table and an opened bottle of red wine with two empty glasses next to it.

"I've learned a lot of things since we were kids," he says with a wink, and it gives me unexpected goosebumps.

"This is awfully nice for a date to watch the evening news," I say, taking a seat at the table. "Can I help you with anything?"

He's standing in front of the stove, stirring something in a pot. I can't see what it is from this angle, but the entire house smells delicious.

"Iris Thornwick, you will sit your butt down and have some wine while I finish this. You're working seven days a week to serve everyone else around here; it's about time you kicked your feet up and let someone serve you."

"Where have you been all my life," I quip, and his response makes my heart flutter.

"Right here."

What is happening? I'm not proud of it, but the thought has crossed my mind that Willow Nora cast some sort of spell or maybe slipped some Love Potion No. 9 in one of our beverages, because how am I getting butterflies over a man I've known this long? How? How!

The realization nearly makes me choke on my wine. The curse. The urban legend, repeated by those old and young for years, that my aunts *were* witches and hated men so much that they cursed any that dare get close to a Thornwick woman. Sure, Mom and I have both been unlucky in love, but I've chosen to believe it's simply because we're too independent for any man to accept. We have our own lives, make our own money, and we don't need a man to save us. The ones around here seem to want a damsel in distress, and that is never a term you'll hear used to describe a Thornwick. Is this man who is falling for me going to be cursed for it? Is he in danger?

They weren't witches, I remind myself. They were teenage girls.

I take another drink to quiet the uneasy thoughts running rampant in my brain.

"I'm surprised you were able to take tonight off with it being the first night of the carnival," I tell Wally. "Don't you need to be on hand in case someone gets drunk and falls off the Ferris wheel?"

He comes over to grab the empty plates from the table and leans his right elbow in front of me. "After nearly twenty years on the force, they finally gave us enough funds to hire someone for Ferris wheel cleanup, so I can take a night off."

Again with the wink. What is happening to me?

"My time is pretty tied up with Kellen's case now. Until I get a solid suspect, I don't think I'll be spending my shifts monitoring the town carnival. Do you want to confess to killing him so I can get some time off?"

He laughs, and I nearly choke on my wine. *Play it cool, Iris.*

"If I'm in jail, how are we going to go to the carnival together?" I ask, tilting my head in a flirtatious way.

"Touché. Maybe hold off on that confession."

Maybe Lucy was right. I'm playing with fire here.

As he's plating up our dinners, I steal a glance at the cluster of framed photos on the wall leading into the living room. The one of Wally's mom holding him as a baby forms a lump in my throat. She was so beautiful, resembling Ann Margaret with her red hair and porcelain skin. The pictures stop for a while after she passed; there are none of him or Rex again until he was in little league. I smile when I see our team picture—Lucy and I were the only girls, and we're both leaning on our bats like some sort of twelve-year-old badasses out to prove our worth. I laugh out loud when I see the framed picture on the far end of the gallery—our tenth grade homecoming picture. He's in a shirt and tie, and I'm wearing a sequined turquoise monstrosity of a dress, with so many bobby pins holding my updo, I lost track at fifty while taking them out that night. I stand to get a closer look.

"That's my dad's favorite picture," Wally says, walking back to the table with our plates. "He sure thinks the world of you. He reminds me all the time that I screwed up my chances with the one who got away."

"Really?" I ask. This is surprising to hear. Rex Parker has always been kind to me, but I sort of got the feeling that he avoided Mom and me over the years because of our family name. The Thornwick case drove him a little mad—all these years and he never got closer to having any answers about what happened to my aunts. The public has not been kind to the man in charge of the investigation. I hope he's finding peace now down at Serenity Assisted Living Home.

"Yeah, he still asks about you. Well, mostly about that banana cream pie you serve at the café, but about you, as well."

I retake my seat at the table and nod approvingly at the dinner he prepared—ribeye steaks, twice-baked potatoes, and sliced carrots with some sort of glaze that smells like brown sugar. I can't remember the last time I had a full meal like this.

"How is he doing down at Serenity?" I ask while cutting into my steak. It's the perfect medium rare. Of course it is.

"Oh, he has good days and bad. The important thing is that he's surrounded by help during the bad days. They can do a lot more for him than I could at home."

"I know you wish you could have kept him here, but you aren't equipped for that level of care. None of us are. He's in the best place, Wally."

He nods in agreement, but I can see his thoughts are listing all the ways in which he feels like he failed his father.

"Speaking of Dad, I need to call the nursing home real quick and make sure they don't have the news on in his room tonight. He has blood pressure issues, and I think that seeing Ann Haven continue to spew her bullshit all these years later might cause him to have a coronary event."

Chapter Twenty-Six

OCTOBER 30TH, 1993

Sarah tucked her long brown ponytail under the baseball cap she fit snugly onto her head. With her dad's faded, oversized Alibi Neighborhood Bar hooded sweatshirt and aviator sunglasses, she was nearly unrecognizable. Which was good, because she was about to go out into a town full of people who would not be very kind if they *did* recognize her.

She slowly crept out of her bedroom and placed her ear against the door of Bridget and Maggie's room. She could hear music playing but no voices, so they were either doing their homework or staring at the wall, like Sarah had been doing in her own room for the past hour.

She tiptoed to the stairwell with her shoes in hand, as to not make any noise. Growing up in this house meant she had the location of every creaky floorboard memorized, so she carefully avoided the few spots she knew would make unnecessary noise. Stopping halfway down the stairs, she could hear her parents speaking in hushed tones, presumably from their bedroom.

"I told you they shouldn't be babysitting for that family," her father said through gritted teeth.

"You can't blame everyone who associates with the Lancasters, or you'd be mad at the entire town, Peter. I don't think the Carters even care for them; they just keep them close because nobody wants to be on their bad side."

This confused Sarah; she'd never seen the Carters associate with Bucky and Brighton Lancaster outside of townwide events that everyone seemed to attend. The Carters were upper middle-class comfortable; the Lancasters were in a different league when it came to their wealth.

Sarah wished she had time to stay and eavesdrop, but she was on a mission and knew she'd have the best chances of sneaking out undetected if she did so while her parents were mid-argument in their room.

She skipped the third-to-last step, which would have made the loudest noise, and landed softly at the bottom of the stairs in her socked feet. She stayed perfectly still for a beat to make sure they hadn't heard her. When they continued to argue, she knew she was in the clear. Tiptoeing down the hall and through the kitchen, she slowly pulled open the back door and crept outside, softly closing it behind her. She slid her feet into her tennis shoes, raised her hood, and hurried to the end of her driveway, turning left as she'd done a hundred times before, in the direction of Ann Haven's house.

Rehearsing her speech as she walked briskly with her eyes focused downward on the cracks in the sidewalk, she began to feel lightheaded. The entire situation was almost too much: She was preparing to confront one of her oldest and dearest friends about what would possess her to give a statement to the police that the Thornwick sisters were practicing witchcraft. It was just so damn ridiculous.

By the time Sarah reached the sidewalk in front of Ann's parents' house, she had a renewed determination to confront her friend and force her to tell the truth. Giving herself one final pep talk, she pulled her sunglasses off, shrugged the hood from her head, and approached the front door. After a few knocks, she could hear Ann's golden retriever, Ollie, barking like the house was under attack. Perhaps he could sense Sarah's intentions.

"Sarah," Mrs. Haven said, pulling the door open slightly. It was quick, but Sarah couldn't miss it: Ann's mom looked happy to see her, which would be her normal reaction, before quickly remembering the situation and shutting down. The woman shook her head. "You shouldn't be here."

"I'd like to talk to Ann. I think she owes me that."

Mrs. Haven looked over her shoulder before closing the gap from the open door until her own face was all that could be seen.

"I know she's in there," Sarah said, stretching her calves to try and get a glimpse over the woman's shoulder.

"She doesn't want to talk."

It was entirely out of character for Sarah to disobey an adult, but you know what they say about desperate times.

"Ann!"

Mrs. Haven jumped at Sarah's booming voice.

"Ann! Come out here—you at least owe me that!"

"It's fine, Mom. I'll talk to her. Just give us two minutes," said Ann, appearing behind her mother.

Sarah was so shocked by Ann's appearance, she nearly reacted out loud. The only time Sarah had seen her friend look so rough was in the ninth grade when she had food poisoning and slept in the bathroom for two days. First, she felt sympathy at the sight, but she quickly remembered what Rex Parker had told them that morning: Ann accused the girls of casting a spell of sickness on her.

"I was about to ask what's wrong with you, but I'm supposed to already know that, since I'm the one who forced this sickness on you with dark magic, right?"

Ann hung her head. Sarah knew that Ann was aware of how ridiculous the words sounded out loud. Slowly raising her gaze to meet Sarah's, her eyes widened as if she remembered forgotten information. Her eyes darted to the left and right of Sarah, checking for anyone else who could be watching.

"You shouldn't be here," Ann told her, crossing her arms. Sarah detected a slight shiver and a row of goose-bumps on her arms.

"Why not? Because you're not ready to be confronted about your horrible lies? Why would you do that to us, Ann? Do you have any idea what the last twenty-four hours have been like for us? They've been hell. Why the fuck would you make that shit up? You know we'd never harm those kids."

She wouldn't make eye contact with Sarah. She couldn't.

"How do you know your sisters didn't do it?"

Something about Ann shifting her story to suggest *only* Bridget and Maggie were involved made Sarah clench her jaw. She could feel her heartbeat in her neck so strongly, she worried it would pound right through her skin.

"What the fuck did you just say?"

"I just—"

"No, you've already tried to ruin our lives. Now you're being confronted about it, so you're going to try and throw my two little sisters under the bus? The ones who didn't leave my side the entire night? The ones who agreed to play your stupid games and who have treated you like a sister for years since you don't have your own? You disgust me."

Sarah turned to leave but stopped to deliver one last line.

"You know, Ann, if I were a witch, I *would* cast a spell on you, but you can bet your ass it would be a lot worse than a little cold. You fucking bitch. Do not ever talk to me again, even when this is over."

As she looked back one final time, she saw Mrs. Haven's face in the window before she let go of the curtain in her hand. She recognized the familiar look in her eyes as guilt. She was allowing her daughter to continue with these accusations, and she knew they were lies, but why?

Chapter Twenty-Seven

Wally is in the kitchen, loading the dishwasher and speaking on his cell phone to the nurse on duty at Serenity to ensure Rex doesn't hear Ann's interview tonight. My mom has already texted me three times, changing her mind about whether she's going to watch it. I know her well enough to know she *will* watch, but it's not going to be pretty. I can't imagine anything Ann could say to change my mom's opinion of her.

"Tonight at six, a town that's been marred by tragedy more than once is once again thrust into the spotlight when the body of a local man was found on the first day of a month-long festival in Westridge Cove. Kellen DeYoung, who was just eight years old when he and several other children famously accused three teenage sisters of witchcraft, was discovered deceased the afternoon of October first. Although the police have yet to release details to the public, local sources have confirmed that DeYoung's body was

"

found hidden in a parade float which appeared in Westridge Cove's opening day festivities."

Hidden? I think while listening to the news anchor. I didn't exactly hide him; I dressed him like a vampire and tied him to a pole on the front of the trailer. It's not my fault his body was surrounded by dummies and may have blended in. In my defense, I thought the axe lodged in his skull might make him stick out a bit, but I was wrong.

"For the first time ever, eyewitness to the original alleged crimes Ann Haven is speaking out about her role in the events that led to the disappearances of three local teenage girls. She's sitting down with Sophia Smith to tell her side of the mystery that rocked the nation back in 1993. We're going to take a quick commercial break and then we'll be back with Sophia and Ann in the studio."

Wally has ended his phone call and joined me on the couch, bringing my half-drunk glass of wine I'd left on the table.

"While they're at it, maybe they should go do some street interviews with these tourists about why even more of them decided to come to the Cove after finding out about Kellen's death. They're morbid. Sick—all of them."

I put my hand on his knee without giving it a second thought.

"I think you may be a little biased because of your connection to this town and to me and my family. Think of Salem, the Amityville house, the scenes of the Manson murders, the house where Jon Benet Ramsey was killed—people have had a morbid curiosity about these places long before my aunts disappeared. If we were two normal people visiting the Stanley Hotel where Stephen King wrote the *Shining* and someone was killed while we were there, tell me there wouldn't be a little bit of curiosity. C'mon, Wally, we'd want to know all the details. It's just hard to understand when it's happening in your own backyard. There's another dead body in everyone's favorite Halloweentown; I get the fascination. It doesn't mean I like it, but I get it."

He places a hand over mine and squeezes.

"You're wiser than I give you credit for."

"If you're just discovering this now, then why did you cheat off my English Lit test in ninth grade?"

Without warning, he leans in and kisses me, catching me so off guard I nearly spill my wine.

"What was that for?" I ask, the fluttering in my stomach intensifying.

"It's just really, really nice to feel this way about someone who also happens to be a friend I've been razzing for thirty years. It's almost too good to be true."

Again, I think of Willow.

"Maybe we've both been through a lot, and the universe just decided we deserve happiness," I suggest.

We kiss again. This one is softer and quicker, but he follows it with a kiss to the tip of my nose and then my forehead.

"And we're back. I'm sending it over to Sophia Smith who is in the studio with Ann Haven, a key player in the nation's favorite unsolved mystery: the Thornwick sisters' disappearance. Sophia, over to you."

We both turn to face the television, unsure of what bombshell Ann is about to drop or, more likely, what new lies she's decided to spew. Here we go.

I have to admit that she looks horrible, and I'd think it even if I didn't despise the woman. She's got makeup layered on an inch thick, but it's not enough to disguise the dark circles under her eyes. Her usually perfectly manicured nails are bare and uneven, as if she's been biting them. Through Wally's high-definition TV, I can even see her dry, jagged cuticles. This is a far cry from the woman we normally see around town, dressing as if her appearance is a direct reflection of her pretentious boutique.

Sophia opens the interview by recapping what transpired in 1993, as if the entire viewing area doesn't already have the details memorized. Everything my aunts did in the last twenty-four hours of their lives has been documented and overanalyzed for years. Down to the brand of coffee my grandma brewed that day (Folgers) to the tennis shoes Sarah was wearing when she ran down the block to confront Ann (Nike), and the friend Maggie usually walked home with (Jessa), there isn't much we don't already know.

Thankfully, they only have an eight-minute slot on tonight's broadcast, so Sophia quickly gets to the point.

"Ann, why now? Why give your first interview in over thirty years? Is it because of the death of Kellen DeYoung; do you fear that you may be next because of your connection to the case?"

The camera focuses on Ann, whose eyes are darting around as if she still hasn't made her mind up about what she's going to say tonight.

"Of course I'm concerned that whoever did this to Kellen is targeting people who were involved in the Thornwick case, but that's not why I chose to come forward today. Kellen was very regretful for any role he may have played in the disappearance of Sarah, Bridget, and Maggie."

I want to reach through the screen and strangle her for thinking she deserves to even speak my aunts' names after what she did.

"I have carried the same guilt for years, and I've been a coward, afraid to come forward about the truth. I was a lost and impressionable girl back in 1993, and I told some horrible lies about three girls whom I loved dearly. Lies that may have cost them their lives," Ann says, barely getting the final word out before a sob escapes her lips. "I've lived with this for so long, and I just can't do it anymore. It's going to kill me if I keep it inside for another day."

"Ann, you were nearly an adult when you made these statements to police, implicating your friends in crimes involving children. You weren't in elementary school like the other accusers. What inspired you to lie to authorities, especially about girls you had been so close to? Did you have a falling out that made you want to seek revenge against them?" Sophia asks, leaning forward, mirroring what we all are doing in our living rooms. It's the question that we've been begging for answers to since the nineties.

Again, she seems unsure before she speaks.

"It's just that . . . uh . . . I was in a bad place. My family was in a bad place. I made some decisions I wasn't proud of. I know they were accused of worshipping Satan, but I think I'm the one who lost my soul to him during that time. I was doing things that were completely out of character for me, and I can't tell you how much I deeply regret my lies."

Sophia waits a moment to see if she's going to continue her explanation before asking further questions. Ann's eyes meet Sophia's, and I can see her silent plea to please understand and cut her a break. Pathetic. Luckily, Sophia is a professional.

"Why did you make the decision, Ann? You still haven't given us a reason."

"I felt immense pressure."

"Pressure? From whom? The boys' parents?"

Ann shakes her head.

"I did what I needed to do for my family."

"How was your family involved, Ann? Are you referring to your parents?"

The corners of Ann's eyes are wet with tears. She continues to shake her head before unclipping the small microphone from the neck of her sweater and tossing it to the side with her battery pack. Her voice is picked up by studio microphones as she mumbles, "I can't do this. It's going to cost me everything. I shouldn't have come here."

Sophia Smith is left looking stunned and alone in an empty studio as Ann Haven slams the door behind her. The broadcast cuts to a commercial. The interview is over.

Chapter Twenty-Eight

PRESENT DAY

Today's low-effort Halloween costume is sponsored by my late night at Wally's (no sex; we were not in the mood for much of anything after that interview, let alone seeing each other naked as adults for the first time) and the fact that Mom and I received no less than three online reviews for the café last night that rated us one-star because they drove all this way to see a Thornwick, and both of us were selfish enough to spend the month in Florida. They came to see the circus, and the monkeys were on vacation. Who cares if the coffee was hot and the loaded potato soup was the best they'd ever had? One star.

Delightful Donuts is my only stop on my way in to work to pick up my usual, along with a black coffee and maple glazed donut for Mom. I glance around the restaurant when I walk in and exhale when I see it's all familiar faces. The donut shop is off the beaten path, and Larry and Fred don't pay for any advertisements in the tourist brochures, so it's a bit of a hidden gem. They've told me their sales double in the month of October, regardless, because so many of us come in seeking refuge from the crowds.

"A *Scream* mask?" Fred says when I pull it off. "Wasn't Nancy just wearing that last week?"

"What do you want from me, Fred? It's hard to come up with thirty-one different masks so we can survive this hell of a month. Sometimes Mom and I share. You wear that apron every day of the week, and you don't hear me yapping about it."

He shrugs and finishes the latte he's making for the customer in front of me; it's one of my neighbor's teenage daughters, but I can't for the life of me remember her name. When he puts a lid on her drink and hands it over, she stops in front of me on her way out.

"I'm sorry you have to wear a mask all month. I'm sorry you and your mom have to go through this every year. I'm just so sorry . . . for it all."

She doesn't wait for a response, which is good, because I find myself a little choked up. She's showing compassion for us, for something that happened before she was even born. I spend so much of this month trying to survive and keep my eye on the end goal, I forget about our neighbors and friends who watch us do this year after year. It must be exhausting for them, as well.

"So," Fred says, leaning forward on the counter and looking both ways before he continues. I know he's about to gossip, and it's such a welcome distraction, I give him my full attention. "So much drama. First Kellen and now Ann. I can't imagine what's going on in that head of yours. We aren't even halfway through October and it's total madness in this town. Maybe we *are* cursed."

Of course I'd like to say, "I killed Kellen myself because that motherfucker had it coming, and if Ann knows what's good for her, she'll be avoiding me after that godforsaken interview," but instead I simply agree with him.

"The only thing going on in this head of mine is that I need to get to work and make enough money so that maybe next year Mom and I will really be on a beach in Florida instead of just pretending we are. I'm so sick of it all, Fred."

"Maybe you're cursed like the Kennedys."

"Nah, they've had far more loss than us. I'm lucky to still have Mom around. We'll get through this month. We always do."

He tilts his head and juts his bottom lip out into a pout, placing a hand over his heart. The best way to describe his current pose would be *demonstrative compassion*.

"I can't imagine what you're going through. Any theories on who the killer might be?"

The worst kind of gossip is that disguised as concern. He doesn't care what I'm going through. He just wants a running theory on what might have happened to Kellen, so he has something to offer the rest of the locals when they come in today. I may be running a little behind for work, but I most certainly have an extra minute to fuck with him.

"Have you considered it's Bucky Lancaster? Who stands to gain the most in this town from the added bloodshed? It makes the most sense, really."

I can practically see his wheels turning as he begins to put together my order.

"Bucky Lancaster, a cold-blooded killer? I mean, he's already cold blooded, so I guess that's half the battle."

"Occam's Razor: The most logical explanation is usually the right one. He owns half the town. The town that makes money every time something fucked up happens here. He has a vested interest in fucked-up things continuing to happen."

"Have you mentioned your theory to Wally?" he says, and judging by the shit-eating grin he's wearing, his big-mouthed partner, Larry, told him about our breakfast date yesterday.

"He's so busy; I wouldn't want to bother him with my silly ideas," I say, batting my eyelashes like a demure lady who can't possibly imagine bothering the man in charge of this town's safety with my foolishness.

"I've got a feeling he'd listen to you," Fred tells me, raising his eyebrows a few times while handing over my bag of donuts.

I'm not going to give him the reaction he's begging for, so I simply stick a few dollars in the tip jar, grab my drinks, and turn to leave with a polite smile on my face.

"See you soon, Fred. Give Larry my best."

I cuss when I realize that I walked from my car to the back door of the restaurant without putting my mask back on. I don't hear any shouts or clicks from cameras, so hopefully I made it inside without detection.

Mom is in the manager's office counting change for one of the servers, and I can hear the unmistakable sounds of a kitchen getting a good old-fashioned ass kicking—timers going off, tickets being printed, orders being shouted, and tongs clapping together. I peek my head in the office to give Mom her coffee and donut.

"You want to talk about Ann?" she asks. "God, this donut smells good. It's just what I needed."

"Let's talk about it after the rush," I respond. We could sit here and overanalyze everything she said during last night's interview, but it's only going to upset both of us and prevent us from doing what we are good at—taking care of our customers.

"Hola, Luis," I say when he passes by the office on his way back to the line.

"Get a more original costume, Iris," he shouts back as he passes by. Why is everyone hating on my *Scream* costume today, but nobody said a damn word when Mom wore it last week?

I'm sure we're doing the same sales volume as yesterday, but something about the vibe seems more chaotic today, more intense. I set my drink on the table designated for employees and head toward the front to see where I'm best needed. (Do *not* let Nancy Thornwick catch you with a drink on the kitchen line. The next line you'll be in is at the unemployment office.)

The kitchen seems to be handling themselves; there's cussing, but it's less than normal and I don't hear anything being slammed or thrown, so I'd say we're doing just fine. Holly is on expo and absolutely killing it; the trays are going out fast and the plate presentation looks beautiful. I make a mental note to talk to Mom about giving her another bump in pay.

Out front, there's a line of customers at the host stand, trying to get their names on the list, and our team of bussers is doing exactly what they are supposed to do—turning tables as quickly as they can, which means pre-bussing dirty dishes as customers finish eating, and wiping and sanitizing everything the second they leave so new customers can be seated. One silver lining about most of our business being from tourists is that they aren't campers; they eat, pay, and go. There is so much to be seen during their day or two in Westridge, they don't waste much time sitting around, especially if they can't catch a glimpse of a Thornwick. The same cannot be said for the twelve seats at the counter, which tend to be filled by locals who don't give a damn how busy we are—they'll stay until they are good and ready to leave.

My heart stops when I see Barrett Carter at the far end, in the last barstool. He has a steaming mug of black coffee sitting in front of him and appears to be alone. He may be a grown man, but from this angle his face looks exactly as it did when we were children. He wasn't a bad kid, and I hate that he grew up to be such an asshole.

Walking behind the counter, I grab the carafe of regular coffee (I've served him enough over the years to know he doesn't drink decaf), and head in his direction. I pretend to be surprised that his mug is full when I get in front of him.

"My bad, I thought you could use a refill," I say, my voice muffled through the tiny hole in my mask.

I pat the counter in front of him before turning around, and he startles me by grabbing my hand before I can leave.

"Iris? Is that you?" he says in a hushed tone.

Yes, it's me. The person you've known your entire life who just killed your best friend and plans to kill you next. In fact, it's taking everything in me not to kill you right now, you worthless son of a bitch.

Instead, I simply nod.

"What are we going to do?" he asks. "I was barely hanging on after what happened to Kellen, and now Ann; it's like someone is seeking revenge for everything that happened back then. Do you think it's a crazed fan?"

"Why is everyone trying to get me to discuss Ann this morning? She did a shitty, attention-seeking stunt on the news last night, and I'm not in the mood to discuss it," I say, leaning forward so the two men next to him can't eavesdrop so easily.

Barrett looks like he's trying to see my eyes through the mask when I see his widen.

"You don't know?"

"I don't know what?" I ask, losing patience.

"Ann Haven is dead. They found her body this morning."

It's the second murder in Westridge this month, but this time, I had nothing to do with it.

Chapter Twenty-Nine

Mom and I are doing what we haven't done since Halloween night last year—sitting on the roof of the restaurant.

It's become a little tradition that stays just between us. There is a small storage closet that you can only access from the roof, and we keep a few folding chairs up here for occasions such as this. Normally, we do it on Halloween night. We climb up the ladder, unfold the chairs, and open a bottle of cheap champagne to celebrate surviving another October in Westridge Cove. Tonight, we're only halfway through the month, but we need the peace and quiet more than ever.

Last night, Ann Haven went on live television to claim that someone coerced her into accusing my aunts of wrongdoing, and she was dead by morning. Mom and I have been through every possibility: the Carters, the DeYoungs, the obvious choice of the Lancasters, since they have more money and influence than anyone else around here. What we can't settle on is a motive. Who in the world wanted to ruin the lives of three innocent teenagers in 1993? Who would stand to gain anything by their disappearances? Who is still around and would want to punish Ann for speaking out? I even asked Mom if Grandma and Grandpa could have been mixed up in anything bad; could they have owed someone money? She assured me that Grandpa worked too much to gamble, and Grandma's biggest wager was a quarter per game when she played cribbage on Wednesday nights. Neither one of them had any known enemies, let alone one angry enough to kill their children.

Sitting up here always makes me feel oddly grateful to live in this community, despite all the reasons I should hate it. We can see the entirety of Main Street from up here, and it looks like the Pinterest search results for "spooky small-town Halloween." Every storefront is decorated for the holiday. Whether it's a few bales of hay adorned with leaves and pumpkins, or businesses like Willow's that go all out with skeletons and a fog machine, it really is a sight to be seen.

The emergence of bloggers and social media influencers certainly has changed the view on a night like this. Years ago, we'd be up here watching kids laughing as they went to each storefront to get a piece of candy, and street performers would offer to let tourists get a picture with their digital cameras. Now, everyone and their brother has a selfie-stick, and they are all "reporting live" from downtown Westridge Cove. A few have even had the nerve to ask that their meals at the café get comped because of their follower count. While desperate for views, they always use buzzwords like "the nation's greatest unsolved mystery" and "a town known for its witches," but this year they don't need the buzzwords. They are in the middle of one of the country's most notorious towns, and two of the key players in the story that made this town famous are now dead. There's a killer on the loose, and nothing could be better for the algorithm this month.

I'm the only one who knows there are actually two killers. Well, Lucy knows, too, but she'd never turn against me.

Mom and I focus on the same man on the street below us, who is being filmed by his friend with a smart phone and a ring light.

"Hey my spooky friends, it's Halloween Harrison, and I'm back with this week's episode of America's Spookiest Towns. I have a feeling this week's video is going to break some records because—you guessed it—I'm in Westridge Cove, Michigan. We're only halfway through October, and there have been two murders in this storied community, and both victims were witnesses in the original case that haunted the nation. Kellen DeYoung and Ann Haven were both murdered by someone who appears to be taking justice into their own hands when it comes to those who were responsible for the disappearance of the Thornwick sisters. Could it be a Thornwick doing the killings? Although it's widely reported that the last two surviving Thornwicks, Nancy and her daughter, Iris, leave town for the month of October, we've received word from a credible source that they are actually both still here in Westridge Cove and have been all month. Come with us while we investigate these crimes and give America the answers they deserve."

As soon as his friend yells "Cut," Harrison is approached by several adoring fans who want selfies, and one teenage girl dressed as Harley Quinn who pulls down the front of her costume and asks him to autograph her bare chest. He gladly obliges. I've never heard of this schmuck, but I have a sneaking suspicion I'm not his target audience.

"Oh, for Christ's sakes," Mom says, taking a sip from her red Solo cup of prosecco. It's the best we could come up with on short notice without going to the liquor store.

"Tell me something about them that I don't remember. Something you've never told me before," I say.

"About my sisters?"

I nod. When I think about how this tiny town ended up a top tourist destination all because of my aunts, it's nearly too much to wrap my head around. We forget—we all forget—that these were three normal teenage girls. I felt the same when I visited Salem for the first time after high school. Every museum, gift shop, tour; they're all named for the witches. But that's the thing . . . They *weren't* witches. They were men and women who were put to death for baseless accusations, and now, just like Westridge Cove, people treat it like a circus attraction. I want to remember the aunts when they were simply three teenage girls in small town America. I want Mom to fill in the blanks in my broken memories from when I was a child.

"Well, Sarah took over the role of being the eldest daughter when I moved out and had you. She took it to an extreme and drove the other two nuts. She always pulled the card of being the oldest and said it was only fair. The thing is, I don't think she had any idea what she wanted to do with her life, and it was starting to stress her out. She was about to graduate and had no plans. I kind of feel like that's why she spent so much time with Willow. Maybe she was hoping that Willow could predict the future or give her some sort of spiritual guidance. I don't know."

I turn my chair slightly to face Mom. I don't want to be distracted by the revelers in the streets. I want to listen to her stories.

"Bridget's goal in life that year was to save up money to

buy a car. It's all she talked about. She turned down invitations to hang out with her friends all the time if an extra babysitting gig popped up. It makes me sick, thinking about how many times she watched you without me paying her for it. The truth is, I just couldn't afford it, and as soon as I started making enough money to compensate them all for watching you, they were gone. Did I ever tell you that Mom and Dad were going to surprise her with a car? He had picked one out down at a local lot and planned to pick it up the first week of November. I wish I could have pitched in for it."

A single tear rolls down her cheek, and she wipes it away before taking another drink.

"You were a young mother who cleaned houses for a living. From what Grandma and Grandpa told me, my aunts loved watching me. They might not have let you pay them, even if you could have. I wasn't a job; I was their niece. Most families don't charge for babysitting, Mom."

She seems to accept this reminder enough to quiet her emotions and tell me about her youngest sister.

"I've told you enough about Maggie's nature because you're so much like her, but the truth is she was the best with you. She adored you. She was always the one to come outside when I'd pull in the driveway to drop you off because she wanted to be the first arms you'd run and jump into. You loved her just as much as she loved you. She was only a kid when you were born, so it was almost like you were growing up together. I'm sure she thought of you more as a little sister than a niece."

Whenever I have flashes of memories from those days, they are almost always of Maggie. I remember she would carry me everywhere, even when everyone else told her I was too old to be carried and needed to walk on my own. I remember the smell of the room she shared with Bridget, although I'm not sure if that memory is coming from all the days I spent there after their disappearance. Maggie had a bottle of Sunflowers by Elizabeth Arden on her dresser, and I used to spray it in the air because it made me think of her. I'd give anything to have more memories of them, but just when I'm focusing hard enough to start to remember, the vision is gone as quickly as it appeared. Occasionally, a smell will drift into my nostrils, and I have no idea where it came from or what it is, but I know it reminds me of my aunts.

"Do you think Grandpa died of a broken heart?" I ask, hoping it's been long enough that she may finally be ready to talk about her father.

"Grandpa's mission in life was to work hard, provide for his family, and keep us safe. It may have been six years later, but there's no doubt in my mind that the stress from losing three of his daughters is what killed him. I wish you could have known them better before everything happened. They were really, really good parents. They loved us so much."

I do have memories of Grandpa, who died when I was twelve, and I have even more of Grandma because she lived until I was in my twenties. They were good grandparents, but the truth is that even as a child, I knew the light was gone from their eyes. I knew they were just going through the motions to get through the day. Everywhere we went, people stared. They kept their distance, as if tragedy was contagious. I'm sure the only reason they stuck around as long as they did was because Nancy needed parents, and they wanted to help with me. The older I get, the more I can't believe they survived it at all. Losing three daughters is unfathomable. Losing them after the entire town falsely accused them of wrongdoing is a kind of grief that is unthinkable. I think the anger alone would have killed me.

"I don't check in with you enough, Iris. I'm sorry."

I let out a little laugh.

"Mom, we work together every day."

She doesn't return the laugh.

"I know that, sweetheart, but we are so busy, we rarely talk about anything besides work and whatever is going on in this town. I'm so consumed with trying to keep this business running smoothly while also thinking about my sisters; I think I've neglected to remember that you've been through the wringer as well. Your life hasn't been easy, especially lately. I'm sorry."

I do what I always do, shake my head, laugh it off, insist I'm okay. Lather, rinse, repeat.

"Tell me something fun. Something to get my mind off all this nonsense," she says.

I hesitate to tell her because I have a feeling that she'll shriek so loud, our secret hiding spot will be detected, but I decide to throw her a bone anyway. She deserves to focus on something other than death. I close my eyes tightly, so I don't have to witness her eruption.

"Well . . . I think I might be in love with Wally Parker."

Reluctantly, I open one eye to see why I haven't heard her react yet. I open the other because I can't believe my eyes. She doesn't look surprised. She takes a sip of her drink and swallows before the corner of her lips curl into a smirk.

"Oh, sweetie, we've all been waiting for this day. Lucy and I had made a bet that you wouldn't holdout past your thirtieth birthdays, but I was wrong. I think you two are the last ones in town to realize that you're in love with each other. I'm just happy you've both put aside your foolish pride and admitted it before it's too late."

Chapter Thirty

OCTOBER 30TH, 1993

When it came to Willow Nora, Sarah thought she hung the moon. She'd spend hours with her after school, soaking up all the information she could from the woman she felt was wiser than any human she'd ever met. Bridget was relatively indifferent about the relationship, and Maggie was the skeptic. She was a logical, grounded girl, and the idea of Willow dabbling in different kinds of magic made her uneasy. Maggie worried about her sister spending so much time in that tiny apartment above Willow's Nook.

By day three of being tormented by the entire town, the girls were willing to try anything. They gladly followed Sarah out their back door to consult with Willow on their predicament.

When they arrived at Willow's shop, they could see nearly a dozen people through the large windows facing Main Street. This is the only week of the year a crowd that size was in a store that was known for oddities and antiques.

About five years prior, Willow made the decision to start selling Halloween costumes, makeup, and accessories, as well, and it certainly helped business this time of year.

"Shit," Sarah said, motioning for her sisters to keep their heads down. "Let's go through the back door; we can wait for her in the office."

"How are we going to get in?" Maggie asked.

"I've got a key," Sarah said with such nonchalance, you'd think every high school senior had the key to a shop owned by the weird old woman in town. "She told me she hired someone to help out this month, so maybe they're here, and she can take a break and talk to us."

The three girls rounded the corner and cut through the alley in back, thankfully undetected. Sarah separated the key from her ring, which also contained a Westridge Cove High key chain, a green rabbit's foot, her house key, and a key to her jewelry box, which also happened to house her diary.

She gently pushed the door open, motioned for her sisters to hurry in, and locked it behind them. Within seconds of entering the dusty back room of Willow's Nook, Bridget was already sneezing.

"Who is back there?" Willow's voice sounded out, with seemingly zero concern that there could be a robbery in progress. She moved the curtain aside that separated the area from the store front and peeked her head through. "Oh, Sarah! Hello! And you brought your sisters. Give me just a second."

All three girls tensed when they heard Willow announce to the store that they had two minutes to make their purchases and leave because she was closing early. Sighs and words of frustration were muttered, but the customers ultimately complied. Within minutes, the girls heard Willow ringing up the final order and turning the deadbolt on the front door. After flipping the sign in the window to Closed, Willow called for the sisters.

"Alright, coast is clear. You girls can come on up here."

Sarah led the pack, pushing her way through the curtains and between the shelves of rubber masks, fake eyelashes, and spray paint made specifically for hair. "Spooky" by Atlanta Rhythm Section was playing on the small radio Willow kept on the counter. It wracked Sarah with guilt that Willow had closed early for them. This was no doubt her busiest day of the year.

"Willow, you really didn't need to close. We could have waited," Sarah told her, keeping her body behind one of the shelves and hidden from street view. Bridget and Maggie followed suit.

"I've had enough business today, and the customers were starting to piss me off. Sometimes sanity is more important than money." Willow hurried to the radio and turned down the volume. "You girls are in a world of shit, from what I hear. Let's go to the reading room."

"I appreciate you, Willow, but I don't think we need our cards read right now. We just need advice," Sarah said with a sympathetic tone.

"I'm not trying to give you a reading, silly girl. I just don't want anyone to see you little satanists through the window and burn my business down for associating with you."

The words caught all three of them by surprise, but the crooked smile on Willow's face after she said them somehow granted the girls a bit of solace, and their shoulders unclenched for the first time that day.

"We're not satanists," Maggie mumbled as they followed the woman through a black door on the far wall, revealing a windowless room with black textured wallpaper and a round table in the center. Six chairs surrounded the table, which was covered in a black cloth with lace detail around the edges. The only light in the room was from an ornate pendent that hung directly over the table. Willow pulled a match from the box sitting on the edge and lit two taper candles, snuggled into antique copper holders.

"I know you're not, my dear. I was just trying to use a little humor. It tends to help in situations such as the one you've found yourself in. Now sit down and tell me everything, girls."

They spent roughly ten minutes telling Willow everything, taking turns while they added more details to demonstrate the ludicrous nature of the accusations. The parents who acted normally when they relieved them of their babysitting duties, only to report them to their mother twelve hours later. The names they were called at school, the prank calls, the eggs being thrown at their house. Finally, the confrontation with Ann, which left Sarah in tears after replaying the conversation.

Sarah had known Willow Nora for years at this point and had not once seen the woman show emotion, let alone shed a tear—for herself or anyone else. It changed that Saturday afternoon when a single teardrop tumbled down her cheek and landed on the table in front of her. She was staring straight ahead, seemingly at the deck of tarot cards stacked neatly in the center of the table, and began fidgeting with the box of matches between her thumb and index finger.

"It's my fault," she said, not breaking her gaze. "It's all my fault."

"How could it be your fault, Willow? You had nothing

to do with this," said Bridget, for once being the sister to speak up.

"If Sarah didn't spend so much time with me, you'd probably never be involved in this nightmare. I've learned that this town tends to hate things they don't understand. It's possibly because they *fear* those things, and deciding to hate is an easier option than admitting they are scared, and they sure as hell aren't going to seek to understand those things they can't seem to get a grasp on. When I opened this shop, and later when my dear Melvin died, the town decided that they didn't understand the things I sold or the way I behaved after his death, so they decided to hate me. They even made up nursery rhymes about how I ate my own husband—did you know that?"

"You didn't?" Maggie asked. Sarah then slapped her arm so hard, she yelped in pain.

"Do you honestly think I'd be spending time with someone who ate her fucking husband, Maggie?"

Willow smiled weakly.

"You remind me of my own sister. She was younger, as well. Sweet as a button but believed everything she heard. No, Margaret, I can assure you that Melvin's remains reside in a beautiful cherry wood urn upstairs in my living room. Although I loved him to pieces, you can rest easy knowing that I've shown no desire to sprinkle him over my dinner like an exotic salt. I can trace the origin of most rumors about me, but I'm still not quite sure where that one came from."

"I'm sorry," Maggie responded sheepishly.

"How do you handle it all?" Bridget asked. She didn't need to explain what she was referencing: How do you handle living in a town where you're gossiped about every single day and they literally clutch their pearls when you pass by? A town where everyone thinks you're different, which must mean you're evil? How do you survive that?

There was a deep pain behind Willow's smile, as she searched for the right words to comfort these poor girls.

"Believe it or not, I used to let it hurt my feelings. I focused so long on the good—the people whose ailments were cured by my remedies, the lost souls who felt peace after I did a card reading, the odd premonitions I've had since I was a kid that have prevented a few tragedies. I couldn't understand how anyone could find ugliness in what I do, and for a while, it nearly broke me."

Sarah seemed the most shocked by this revelation; she couldn't fathom Willow ever being fragile enough to get her feelings hurt. She had nerves of steel. She always seemed to let the chatter simply roll off her back, and she did it with a wicked smile. It's what Sarah admired most about her.

"Then, I noticed something strange; each time the heat turned up in town because there was a new rumor about me, my store got busier. They said I was casting spells and contacting spirits, and suddenly my books on occult started flying off the shelves. I couldn't order enough to keep in stock. I increased the price of my Ouija boards by twenty percent because I was selling so many. One time I ordered some vintage-looking brooms from a wholesaler and accidentally received one hundred, rather than the ten I thought I was ordering. I started the rumor about me being a witch myself, just so I could sell them all. It worked," she said with a wink. "People couldn't wait to buy a broom from an actual witch. Thank goodness they didn't see the shipment box and learn they were manufactured in China. This town may try to break me, but they're also paying my bills every month, which makes the situation a little easier to accept."

This got a laugh from all three girls. It felt good to laugh, something they hadn't done since this all began, just days ago, but it somehow felt like it had been much longer.

"You can't control what people in this town say about you; you can only control your response. My advice? This will all blow over, so you might as well lean into it and have a little fun."

Chapter Thirty-One

PRESENT DAY

"Have you texted him to ask if there are any leads? Do we know how she died?" Lucy asks, kicking off her dress shoes in the entryway and throwing her tweed blazer on the chair in our living room. She may have a grown-up job now, but she still behaves like a messy teenager.

"I just texted him to tell him that I know he's had a busy morning and I'm thinking of him. He just hearted the message, but he hasn't replied."

Lucy collapses on the couch beside me and kicks her feet up on the coffee table, another thing I've asked her to stop doing, but I don't currently have the energy to fight with her.

"And you're sure you didn't do it?" she asks, looking me straight in the eyes because, like I said earlier, she's a human lie detector when it comes to me.

"Lucy, really? Why the fuck would I kill Ann? I mean,

I've definitely daydreamed about it after what she did to my aunts, but why wouldn't I have done it years ago?"

"A few months ago, I didn't think my best friend would be capable of killing *anyone*, but here we are. You used to cry when we'd see a dead deer on the side of the road, and now you're a homicidal maniac. Hey, wait—do you think you might have a brain tumor? I was watching this show, and this guy started acting insane, and it turns out he had this tumor the size of a baseball in his head that was causing his personality to change."

I open my can of sparkling water, and I'm already annoyed because I'm drinking sparkling fucking water instead of a Diet Coke because I'm trying to be healthier, so I take a long inhale and exhale before responding.

"I don't have a tumor, Lucy. I'm not crazy. I'm just a woman who is hellbent on revenge. You were on board with this when I started; I'm not sure what's changed."

"What's changed is that you're killing people you're personally connected to, which is how people get caught. I don't want to have to visit you in prison. I'm too pretty; I'd have a girlfriend in there before anyone gave you a second look."

"I'm not going to get caught."

She opens her mouth to argue but thinks better of it and sinks back into the couch.

"How was work today? You get anything other than a paycheck in exchange for selling your soul?" I ask, trying to change the subject.

"Iris, I couldn't be a server forever. You need to quit holding this over my head."

I know that Lucy wasn't going to work for us forever, no matter how badly I wanted her to.

I just never imagined she'd accept a position working for the Lancasters.

I'll never forget the day she showed up for her shift at Thornwick Café ten minutes early; honestly, that's when I should have known something was up. She was the queen of showing up thirty seconds before she was due to clock in, with an iced coffee in her hand and a protein bar hanging from her mouth while apologizing like it was her first time.

She asked if Mom and I could go in the office and have a chat with her before our shift started, which was also new. Whatever she had to say to us could usually be said anywhere, especially since our entire staff was like family.

"Hey, Lucy Goosey, what's on your mind?" my mother had asked, as we all stayed standing in the cramped office.

"Nancy, you know you're like a mother to me," Lucy started.

"And I love you like a daughter. Nothing could change that. Whatever you're about to say, just say it. We both love you very much."

That's the thing about my mom—she always knows the right thing to say. She always leads with love. She was dealt such a rough hand in life, and she's not once let it affect her optimism or kind nature. The older I get, the more I realize how lucky I am. Lucy has been lucky to have her, as well— she's saved her from more than one bad situation over the years.

"I'm taking a job working for Lancaster Enterprises."

Mom and I spoke at the same time, her saying, "Oh, my," and me scoffing, followed by, "Are you fucking kidding me?"

"You said you guys loved me no matter what," Lucy said, directed at me.

"That was Mom; I didn't say shit."

"Iris Elizabeth," my mom said, scolding me like she did when I was a kid.

"Fine," I said. "I do love you, but I also think you're a fucking idiot. You've got it made here; you basically make your own schedule, you make great tips, and you don't have to worry about work when you go home. What are you unhappy about?"

The look she gave me after those words is what killed me; it was pity. Pity for me because I couldn't possibly understand how she could want more than this.

"I'm not unhappy, Iris. I just want to challenge myself. All I've ever done is work in this restaurant, and it's been twenty years. You know I've always been interested in real estate, and when Brighton and the other ladies came in last week, she mentioned a paid internship that Lancaster Enterprises had open and that she thought I would be perfect for it."

"An internship? You're not eighteen anymore, Lucy," I said, causing Mom to once again scold me. "Are they going to pay you in iced coffee and IOU's?"

"Once I went in and met with Bucky, he offered me an actual position in the office, not just an internship."

"I can't believe while we were here slaving away over a hot stove, you were having cocktails with Butthole Bucky. You're despicable."

"We didn't have cocktails, and you've never slaved over a hot stove a day in your life. Have you lost your mind? You're behaving like a child, Iris."

It took ten minutes for Mom to calm me down enough to apologize to the best friend I've ever had. It took another day or so for me to accept that it wasn't a prank and she was really leaving us to go work for the Lancasters. It took weeks after she left for me to stop checking for her coat on the rack when I clocked into work. It's been over a year now, and I'm finally ready to admit that she's the best employee the café has ever had, and I can't believe we are surviving a second October without her beside us.

"I'm surprised you're sitting here on the couch with me. Don't you need to hop on your computer and do some facts and figures? Put in a little overtime for the man?"

She kicks my leg.

"Facts and figures? It's been over a year; do you even know what the hell I do, Iris?"

"You work for an asshole. I don't need to hear the ins and outs of it."

"That asshole has raised a lot of money to fund a memorial statue in honor of your aunts."

After watching Ann's interview, I can't help but wonder if he's funding that statue because of the guilt he feels over pressuring her to lie about Sarah, Bridget, and Maggie. Who else would be powerful enough to convince a teenage girl to throw her best friends under the bus? I've got to figure out how to prove it was him. I'm not sure where to begin, but what I *am* sure of is that when it comes to revenge, I never give up. I'm not sure if it will take days, months, or years, but I'm coming after you, Bucky Lancaster.

Chapter Thirty-Two

PRESENT DAY

Although it hasn't yet been announced to the public, Wally let me know this morning that the medical examiner believes Ann was poisoned. Judging by the presence of foaming at the mouth, and piles of vomit surrounding her body, combined with the lack of any obvious physical injuries, all signs are pointing to her ingesting something that ultimately killed her.

He said it's not going to be easy to prove someone did this to her. She could have taken her own life after admitting she'd been lying about my aunts for decades. The medical examiner has a long road ahead before he can compile all the evidence, including her stomach contents and official time of death. As Wally was explaining the complicated nature of the case to me, I couldn't help but wonder why I didn't choose to just poison my victims. It would have been a lot easier to get away with it, but it wouldn't have near the level of pizazz as throwing a body from the cliffs or hanging one on display during the town parade. I guess I could use poison as a plan B in the future. I drugged both victims before I killed them anyway. What's a few extra pills crushed up in their drinks? Maybe a little rat poison in their soup? My wheels are turning.

Today I'm wearing a Rainbow Brite costume, complete with the blue dress, multicolored, striped socks, and a plastic mask that would appear to have a pretty ominous smile if it weren't inspired by a children's cartoon.

"Excuse me, miss?" a customer asks as I've just passed by their table. The best thing about wearing a mask, other than hiding my identity, is that I don't actually have to wear my fake customer service smile when interacting with the public. Anyone who has ever worked in hospitality knows the smile I'm referring to. It can be exhausting.

"Yes, sir?" I respond in my slightly high-pitched and friendly customer service voice, which I do still have to use. My mom tends to frown upon me using my usual dry, sarcastic tone.

"Will there be mosquitos at the carnival tonight? My wife is allergic. She swells up like a balloon."

I turn my attention to the wife, who shrugs and gives me a *gee shucks, I sure am a hassle, but he loves me* smile.

These are the moments, the ones where our first reactions play in our heads before we remember where we are and how we should respond.

What I think is *Yes, sir. I'm so glad you asked because I am actually related to the person who controls the mosquitos in town. I'll make sure and put in a call to make sure he has them turned off tonight, just for your wife.*

What I actually say is "Ahh, so you've heard about our state bird, the mosquito?"

Pause for laughs . . . I fake laugh with them . . . and continue.

"Although northern Michigan can be a little *pesty* when it comes to bugs, you've come at a great time. Anything that can bite you is normally gone by this time of year, and the lot where the carnival takes place is far enough from the water that mosquitos don't tend to be a problem. The carnival is a lot of fun; I think you both will have a great time. Be sure to get one of Auntie Dee's famous elephant ears; they are so delicious, you'll want to come back for another one before you leave town."

This seems to satisfy him, as he gives his wife a smile that says *see, honey, I told you I'd take care of those mosquitos for you.*

But, as I turn to leave, he stops me with another question. This time, he lowers his voice, but only slightly.

"So, you work for the Thornwick women? What is that like?"

I collect myself. I get asked this question every October. This time is no different.

"They are wonderful employers. I really enjoy my job."

"How long have you worked here?" the wife asks. She's wearing a Bar Harbor, Maine shirt which tells me they will probably head to one of Bucky's tacky T-shirt shops before they leave town to get their obligatory souvenir.

"Over twenty years," I say, which happens to be the truth.

Their eyes grow wide.

"Wow, that's a long time. I hope they didn't cast a spell on you to make you stick around this long," he says, laughing hysterically at his quip.

I don't have the energy to match his laughter.

"Well, at least they picked a spell that will make me some money," I say, then turn on my heels and walk away before they can respond.

I stiffen at the sound of commotion near the entrance to the restaurant, but unclench my jaw when I see it's just the normal chatter surrounding Butthole Bucky Lancaster's arrival. He doesn't come here much because Brighton is making him watch his sodium intake, but today's special is the Thai Chicken Wrap, which happens to be his favorite, so I had a feeling we'd be graced with his presence.

"Mayor Lancaster, welcome in. It's good to see you," I say, walking past the host stand. "Mindy, you can give him the far seat at the counter while he waits for his to-go order."

"Iris, I'd recognize that voice anywhere. I see you and your mother are serving plenty of tourists this week. Is everything going well?"

He is wearing the absolute dumbest fur hat. It reminds me of Cousin Eddie on *Christmas Vacation* when he's emptying the shitter.

"Thank you for asking; we're having a fantastic week, despite the tragedies."

His facial expression changes immediately with my words, as if he's just now remembering he's supposed to be mourning two members of his community instead of cele-brating the increased business their deaths have brought. He tightly nods and tips his dumb hat before I turn to head back to the kitchen. I really wish my mother was around to witness that polite interaction; she would have been quite proud of me.

When I return from checking on the cook line and expo station, I emerge behind the fully packed counter to see Bucky sitting where I instructed Mindy to send him. He's planted on a stool, hunched over and most likely checking emails on his phone or pretending to, and he's in the exact same seat Barrett Carter occupied just yesterday. Two men who I plan to kill in the very near future, enjoying the same seat in my family's restaurant. This world is just filled with coincidences.

Chapter Thirty-Three

PRESENT DAY

By the third week in October, we haven't had a single employee at the restaurant call out this month, which means that everyone is making money. If you've managed a restaurant before, you know how slow business days tend to inspire flu symptoms.

Mom and I started a system this year where we give a percentage of sales to the cooks, dishwashers, hosts, and bussers so that they do better when we do better. It seems to be working; morale is a lot higher than it was last year, and I may even be able to take a full day off today because every position is covered. Mom will work a double to make sure everything is going smoothly, and I'll return the favor for her tomorrow so she can take a full day off. Who would have ever thought that one twenty-four-hour period without working would feel like a vacation?

I'm starting the day with a long bubble bath because . . . well, why not? My feet and my back are both aching, so I go a little heavy on the Epsom salts and throw back a few Aleve tablets. Lucy is at work and so is Wally, but he's promised to cut out early so we can have a night at the carnival together before its two-week run is over. I mentioned us going together as a half-assed joke, but I'm secretly excited that he managed to get a few hours off so we can act like tourists and check it out. I promised my friend Kayla that I'd help set up her haunted corn maze after she let me know that they had plenty of event volunteers but not nearly enough to set up before open. Every year, I wish I could be one of the "professional scarers" she employs to hide in the corn fields and jump out at screaming tourists, but there's simply too much going on at the restaurant to commit to something like that. I did offer to help hang décor and plan out the map of paid villains while I'm off today, which she seemed thankful for. She let me know that Barrett Carter would be one of the volunteers today, which cemented my decision to make an appearance.

I'm climbing out of the bath and reaching for a towel when I trip over my own foot and slam into the medicine cabinet above the toilet. I don't use it much because I have a vanity in my room, so when the door flies open, it's mostly filled with Lucy's belongings.

When I reach forward to stand her fallen perfume bottles back up, a couple of items catch my attention—a high-dose sleep aid (which Lucy doesn't take) and a prescription bottle for triazolam, which is a sedative. The label is torn off, so I can't see who it was prescribed to. There's also a small, blue plastic contraption that I believe is a pill crusher because it looks like one my grandmother had. Lucy sleeps like a baby and doesn't suffer from any sort of anxiety like the rest of the world, so I can't imagine why she'd have these bottles. Unless her train of thought was similar to mine after she'd heard about Ann's cause of death;

maybe she's doing a little wishful thinking that I'll discover a less violent way to carry out my revenge tour. I vow to have patience when she pitches the idea for me to start overdosing my victims, rather than strangling them or throwing them off cliffs. I'll chat with her about it tonight when I'm back from the carnival and she's home from work.

I rifle through my storage box of Halloween costumes and masks to find an option for the corn maze setup, allowing my face to breathe while also protecting my identity. I have an entire stack of plastic masks with tiny white strings that wrap around my head to secure them in place. Although they are stiff, my skin can breathe a lot easier than when I wear the thick, sweaty rubber masks. I dig until I find one that is a wrinkly old man and smile. Mom wore it one year for Halloween after we'd closed down the restaurant and headed to a locals-only after-party at town hall. She wore a trench coat with it and none of us, myself included, could believe our eyes when she opened the trench coat to reveal a skin-colored bodysuit, adorned with an incredibly realistic piece of male anatomy hanging from the front. My sweet, innocent mother dressed as a geriatric streaker, and I don't think we ever recovered from the shock. Lucy laughed so hard she cried, and I even recall Bucky Lancaster smiling and shaking his head. Nancy Thornwick has been known to throw a few curveballs over the years.

While I won't be attaching a rubber penis to my costume, I do grab a matching Adidas tracksuit I've had since college and throw it on with some tennis shoes in a similar shade. I tuck my hair into a tight twist, grab a newsboy cap from Lucy's room, and pull the mask on. Voila! Anonymous elderly man.

Before I leave our apartment, I circle back to the bathroom and shake out a handful of pills from the bottle of sedatives into my hand. I'm sure Lucy won't mind if I just tuck them in my pocket for assistance. I've got a big to-do list today, and it needs to be finished by five when Wally gets off work.

I smile when I pull off the county road and onto the driveway to Kayla's family farm. There's a new sign this year and it reads KAYLA'S HAUNTED KORN MAZE in haphazard, ominous font on a large wooden sign, hung slightly off-center on a pole shortly after you pull in. There is red paint dripping from each of the letters in a blood-like manner and a large arrow pointing down the driveway. As my car crawls up the drive at a snail's pace, I take in all that she's already put up—scarecrows, bales of hay, signs to turn around before it's too late. You get the gist. The tourists are going to be beside themselves with joy over this whole scene.

Her brother, who runs the farm during normal operating hours, is bent down plugging in what appears to be either a strobe light or fog machine beside the driveway. Both of the family's yellow labs are at his side until they see me and let out a few barks. I roll down my window and put the car in park.

"What's up, Ben?"

He scrunches his nose and squints in my direction. *Fuck, my mask.* I pull it up, exposing my face.

"Iris Thornwick. I thought you were just another old man coming over here to harass me," he says with a smile that would have drove me wild in high school, but my childhood crush dissipated when he grew to be a complete dickhead in our twenties.

"No such luck," I reply. "Just stopped by to help Kayla with setup. Is she around?"

He nods and motions toward the smaller of two barns,

where she typically sets up a hot chocolate and caramel apple station, close to the exit of the maze.

"Hey," he says, as I put my car in drive. I slow down before I'm out of earshot. "What's this I hear about you and Wally Parker?"

"Does this town have nothing better to do than gossip? We've got two dead bodies, and all you guys want to do is talk about who might be fucking."

Normally, he'd throw a barb right back at me, but instead he just pulls his lips into a tight smile. "Maybe some of us are just happy that there's something positive to talk about around here."

Okay, I take back what I said. Maybe he didn't grow up to be a *total* asshole.

"I've been spending some time with Wally, yeah," I admit.

"It's about time, Iris. God knows you both deserve the happiness."

For once, I don't sense sarcasm in his tone.

"Thank you, Ben. I really appreciate that."

I continue down the drive and pull in front of the small barn, with both labs running up behind my car and waiting for me to get out.

"Hi, Pacey; Hi, Minnie," I greet the dogs, both of whom I've known for years. I pick up a stick nearby and throw it into the field, which causes both to go sprinting after it. I wish I had time to have a dog, but with mine and Lucy's work schedules, the poor thing would be couped up in the apartment all day.

"You came," Kayla says, walking out of the barn toward my car.

"A woman is only as good as her word, and I said I'd be here," I reply, giving her a hug.

"I know it's a tough month for you, and I sure appreciate your help. Judging by the number of responses we got from our Facebook post, it's going to be a crazy two weeks here at the farm."

I look between the two barns, toward the entrance to the maze, and see at least a dozen people carrying dummies, scarecrows, and a giant cross made from stalks of corn. She notices my reaction to the cross.

"We're going full *Children of the Corn* this year, cross scene and all."

"Who's going to play the victims? Are they going to have to stay up there all night? I couldn't love this more. That's one of my favorite movies."

"No," she says, smiling and smacking my back like it's a silly question. "We've got plenty of fake bodies to secure up there. I bought a whole load from a Halloween store in Wisconsin that went out of business last year. The plan is to have so many of them placed throughout the maze, people won't know which ones are real. It's going to be insane this year."

She's making it too easy for me. She's practically begging me to hide a body in here. I reach my hand into my right pocket to feel for the pills; still there.

"Tell me where I can help you the most for the next three hours," I say.

"Three hours? You have to go into work tonight?"

I shake my head and smile.

"Wally Fucking Parker," she says, returning the smile. "It's about damn time."

"Yeah, that's what I keep hearing."

"Well, if you want to get to work on these dummies, most of them already have dried blood and some sort of axe or weapon coming out of their heads, but if they don't already look dead, I have a bunch of props and paint on the table next to the entrance. If you would just start walking the maze and placing them wherever you think will scare the shit out of these tourists, that would be great. I've got a map on the table of where the live performers will be hiding throughout the maze, so you can avoid those spots. Most of them should be in there setting up their scare spots already, so let me know if you have any feedback."

"Will do," I say with a wink and head toward the maze.

I pull my mask down as I approach the rest of the volunteers. Although I know most of the guys, I don't need any of them remembering a conversation with me today. I'm taking inventory of the fake bodies and props when I hear two men talking by the entrance about securing a ring of fire over the entry way arch this year. They are debating the logistics, so I glance at the map, see where Barrett Carter is assigned, and sneak past the men unnoticed.

After passing a few teenagers testing out their chain-saws, followed by three guys plotting out their demented clown dance routine and a gaggle of girls perfecting their haunted doll poses, I find myself alone in the maze. I have one dummy under each arm, and they are much lighter than I expected. In fact, once I'm certain that I'm alone, I begin to skip to my destination. The skipping inspires me to whistle one of my favorite songs, "Daydream" by the Lovin' Spoonful. What a beautiful October afternoon it's turned out to be.

Chapter Thirty-Four

PRESENT DAY

There's something about the Westridge Cove Carnival at night that even I can appreciate. Wally and I are walking from his house, since it's only blocks away, and the sounds as we approach are pure joy—children laughing, buzzers sounding from the carnival games, generic music from the rides, and ghostly howls from the tinny speakers outside the haunted house. Trust me, I considered killing Barrett in the haunted house for dramatic effect, but it would be too hard to do it unnoticed, and the maze was the only place I knew he'd be alone at a certain time. As it turns out, premeditated murder is all about logistics.

"How was work?" I ask, my pinky skimming his hand a few times as we walk beside each other.

"Oh, you know. Running our own version of Halloweentown while investigating two murders has been keeping me busy. It's been hell, but it's given me a mental break from the usual."

"What's the usual?"

"You," he says, grabbing my hand. "I don't know what's happened, but you're all I can fucking think about. It's hard to focus."

I once again think about Willow. I swear to God, if she put a damn spell on us to fall in love, I'm going to kill her. We haven't even slept together yet, so it's not like I'm getting laid too much to think logically.

"Yeah. I've been thinking about you all day, too. What has happened to us?"

"I'm not sure, but I had to stop at the nursing home to see Dad today, and half the women working there gave me some version of 'it's about time' when I walked in. Other than us, nobody seems surprised about this."

I let go of his hand to pull my mask down once we are within a block of the carnival. I can't risk ruining this night with news that Iris Thornwick was spotted.

"I've been getting the same response. I guess we really were the last two to find out."

We walk a few more steps before I ask the question I've been avoiding at all costs.

"How was he today—your dad?"

"This new doctor seems to agree that his traumatic brain injury is what caused the dementia to progress so rapidly. It's hard not to be angry about it all, so I just trust that this universe has a plan and this is part of it. Doesn't make it any easier, but it calms my rage a little. I know you can understand that."

If he only knew how much rage I still have running through these veins.

"I sure do," I lie.

"So, what's on the top of Iris Thornwick's carnival must-haves?" he asks, a welcome change to the subject.

"I mean, obviously an elephant ear. And we've got to do the haunted house because I saw the entry fee is being donated to the animal shelter this year. Oh, and maybe we could play the squirt gun horse race game? Remember when I kicked your ass in high school and you had to lie about why you didn't win?"

He gasps, and it absolutely sends me over the edge to see how mad he still is, twenty years later.

"Iris, you cheated. Not only did I have something in my eye—which I told you so we could hold on a fucking minute before starting—but you lied and said that my dad was arresting our math teacher so I would turn and look. Your little horse was halfway down the track before I even turned back around. I can't believe you call that a victory, you dirty little cheat."

By now, I have tears rolling down from the corners of my eyes, so I quickly lift my mask to wipe them away.

"Stay mad, Parker," I say as we approach the ticket booth.

"Hi, Donna," Wally says to Donna Paisley, volunteer ticket booth worker and town gossip.

"Hi Chief Parker and—" She leans forward and whispers, "Iris Thornwick."

She quite literally squeals with glee while clapping her stubby little hands together, nails clacking.

"I just *knew* you two would end up together. It just took some time. Lord knows you both deserve to be happy after all you've been through."

Wally puts a hand on my back, and I'm sure it seems like a sweet gesture to Donna Paisley, but I know he's doing it as a reminder that I need to holster my smart mouth. He and Lucy can read me like a book, I swear.

"Thank you, Donna," I say in my customer service

voice. "We are so happy to have found love right down the street from each other. Who would have guessed, after all these years?"

With this she squeals again. I've given her just what she wanted to hear. Within five minutes, half the town will be involved in some sort of group text where Donna gets the credit for officially confirming our romance. Wally pays her for both of our admissions and we walk away, his hand still on my back.

"So, you love me? Isn't it a little early for the L-word?" he says, pulling his arm down and elbowing me.

"Oh, pipe it. I was just giving the woman what she wanted to hear. I think you're alright at best."

We both smile because we know that's a lie.

Wally is in a hooded sweatshirt from the Great Lakes Fishing Tournament he won last summer, and it's the perfect disguise for the tourists. They know him by name, but most wouldn't recognize him out of uniform.

"I suppose we kind of confirmed this thing without actually talking to each other about it. I hope you're feeling okay about that," he says as we walk side by side to the haunted house.

"This thing?"

"You . . . me . . . you know," he says, motioning back and forth between us.

He's so cute when he's flustered.

I have to remind myself I'm talking about Wally Fucking Parker. Again.

"I'm okay with it if you are," I say, bumping him with my hip as we take our places in a long line, which makes me happy for the animal shelter and all the funds they'll be receiving at the end of the week.

"I'm over the moon about it. And when October is over

and life calms down a little, I'd love to take you somewhere. I think we could both use a little getaway to clear our heads."

I couldn't agree more, but I'm not going to plan that trip yet because my new boyfriend is going to have a few more murders to solve before the month is over. Who knows when his schedule will clear up again?

Chapter Thirty-Five

OCTOBER 30TH, 1993

The girls made their way back home from Willow's, hoods pulled up securely and eyes aimed at the sidewalk each time a car passed by. As they neared the house, they were all happy to see Iris on the front lawn, playing squirt gun battle with Wally Parker. The kids didn't immediately see the Thornwick sisters, so they continued their mock war with kicked up leaves, direct sprays to the head, and typical shouts of battle in a fight between two six-year-olds. The girls laughed out loud when they overheard Iris threatening to bury Wally's body at sea.

"Whoa, whoa, that's probably enough battle for today," Maggie said, dropping her hood and jogging to meet the kids.

"Maggie!" they shouted in unison. Iris ran into her arms while Wally stood in place with raised fists, celebrating the arrival of his favorite babysitters.

"Where's your mom? In the house?" Sarah asked as she caught up to the scene.

The front door opened, with a panicked Sheila Thornwick rushing outside.

"Where have you girls been? I've been worried sick about you. With everything going on, you have to tell us when you're leaving the house. No excuses."

"We just went for a walk to clear our heads," Sarah responded before the other girls had a chance to stumble through a lie. Her mother had no real issue with Willow Nora, but after this week's events, she might suggest the girls keep their distance from the only other person in this town to be accused of witchcraft.

"Your sister is worried sick about you. She came to see you and dropped Iris off so she could go clean a few houses. She'll be back to get her tonight, and I suggest you three are around when she arrives," Sheila said, crossing her arms, one of which was holding a kitchen towel. "Everyone come inside now; I've made Halloween cookies, and they are just about to come out of the oven."

Only Sheila Thornwick would be baking cookies whilst in the middle of personal turmoil. Both kids cheered and ran inside, with the girls following closely behind.

"What's up with Wally?" Bridget whispered to her mother.

"Rex had to work and didn't know who else to call. Lucky for us, he's the only one who doesn't think you sweet girls are practicing witchcraft, so your babysitting gig is secured," Sheila whispered back.

Bridget shrugged. *Fair enough*, she thought. *At least someone in this town still wants to hire us.*

Sheila pulled the cookies out of the oven and lectured everyone on waiting until they cooled down so they wouldn't burn themselves. There was a knock at the door, and as soon as Sheila left the kitchen to answer it, every person in the room disobeyed her and grabbed a cookie.

"They are ghosts; that's spooky," little Wally Parker said as he blew on his cookie before eating it.

Maggie smiled as she watched Iris mimic Wally and blow on hers. They were so impressionable at that age.

"I'm eating a pumpkin one because that's less spooky," Iris said, proud of herself for making such a decision.

Sheila came back in the kitchen, slamming a pile of pamphlets on the counter. It only took reading the headline to know what they were—religious material. An entire stack, delivered right to their door.

Sarah walked over to the pile and thumbed through them. "Is Satan Tempting You?" "It's Not Too Late to Commit Your Life to Jesus!"

Wouldn't you know it, all they'd have to do is show up to this church and pledge ten percent of their household income to the pastor and they'd earn a spot in heaven. Such a simple solution for three wayward daughters.

"Why are you all sad?" Iris asked, taking an oversized bite of her cookie, crumbs tumbling down the front of her orange Halloween sweatshirt and onto the kitchen table. It was amazing what children could pick up on; they'd all tried to put on brave faces in front of the kids, but they were more intuitive than the girls gave them credit for.

"They are sad because everyone found out they are witches," Wally answered matter-of-factly before hopping off his chair to get another cookie from the cooling rack.

"Why would you say that, Wally?" asked Sheila, careful not to use a stern tone and scare him off from telling the truth.

"Barrett Carter said his mom told him that our babysitters are really witches and they just have to hide it sometimes. But at night they fly over our houses on brooms, and they take children who have been bad."

"If that's the truth, why aren't you afraid of us?" asked Bridget.

"Because I'm not bad, and even if I was, I know you wouldn't hurt me."

Something in Maggie broke when Wally said those words. Of course they'd never hurt him. They'd never hurt anyone.

Chapter Thirty-Six

PRESENT DAY

"Iris Thornwick, you are glowing. What the fuck happened?" I can't help but blush when Lucy confronts me with this question as I walk in the door to our apartment, so I deflect.

"Me? Lucy Edwards, what the fuck happened to *you*?"

She hops to her feet from her spot on the couch and squints her eyes.

"Did you get laid?"

I gasp in mock horror.

"How dare you," I shoot back before we both collapse on the couch together in a fit of laughter. "Believe it or not, we haven't slept together. I just had a really good time with him at the carnival, and I didn't get recognized once. It was fantastic. I felt like a normal person."

I lean my head back and replay several moments from tonight's date—screaming and grabbing onto Wally's arm in the haunted house, putting my head on his shoulder on the Ferris wheel, laughing so hard we cried as we finally had a rematch on the squirt gun pony race game (I let him win), and sharing an incredibly sweet kiss at the end of the night when he walked me to my car, parked in his driveway. It just felt so good to put all my worries aside for a night. I must be reminiscing too long, because Lucy coughs to get my attention.

"Huh?"

"Iris, my friend, you are officially smitten. I've never seen you like this over a guy, let alone one you haven't even slept with. I take back what I said before. Maybe this is a good idea. Maybe you could just chill out on your vengeance tour? Find some other way to seek revenge? Like maybe one that wouldn't give you twenty-five to life?"

I consider her words before answering. I don't want to argue with Lucy, but there's no way in hell I'm stopping now.

"My list is almost complete, and I promise you, I'll be done. Nobody will ever find out it was me, and then Wally and I can live happily ever after, and you can be the maid of honor. No more murders for the rest of my days."

My stomach turns when I realize she doesn't know about Barrett Carter. Judging by the lack of news, nobody does. I hope the crows aren't pecking at his body by now.

"Just don't make me wear an ugly dress," she responds.

"That's a promise," I say, reaching my pinkie out to lock with hers. "Have you eaten yet? All I had was an elephant ear and I'm all sugared up. I need some meat."

She releases her pinkie from mine and fist bumps me. "That's my girl. Let's go get some meat!"

"How about the Thai place?" I suggest. "They are staying open until midnight all month for to go orders; I heard someone talking about it at the carnival."

"Hell yeah. Keep that mask with you just in case. Actually, put it on regardless; I'd love to start a rumor that I'm hooking up with a wrinkly old man."

"I already started that rumor about you when you started working for Butthole Bucky," I say with a wink.

I get to my feet before I lose ambition. Thai food sounds amazing, but I'm also exhausted.

"Get in the car, asshole. And for the record; he's not wrinkly. He takes great care of his skin for a man his age."

"Yuck," I respond, mostly to be childish.

I drive the three miles to Thai Kitchen, during which Lucy changes the music about thirteen times, which she knows drives me absolutely insane.

"Maybe we could just drive in silence," I suggest.

"Maybe you could shut the fuck up and let me find something good on your playlist."

"I'm telling my mom you talked to me like that," I threaten.

"She'd never believe you," she says, propping the back of her hand under her chin like an innocent child. She's right; Lucy is like the golden child in Mom's eyes. She can do no wrong.

We pull into an angled parking spot in front of the restaurant and simultaneously cuss when we see the queen-bee bitches of Westridge Cove through the window: Brighton Lancaster, Carol Carter, Karen DeYoung, and another woman from their Junior League group whose name we can't recall because they never allow her to speak. I'm like ninety-eight percent sure it's Lana. Joining their table from the restroom is Callie DeYoung, Kellen's widow and Karen's daughter-in-law.

"Fuck my life," Lucy says. "I cannot deal with those bitches tonight."

The women are at the first table when you walk in, so there's no way to avoid them.

"Well, shit. I'll do it, but I'm going to wear my mask."

"You don't think they'll recognize you?" she asks.

"They each have a half-filled cocktail in front of them with an empty pushed to the edge of the table. I'd guess they're drunk and too preoccupied with whatever they're gossiping about to notice someone with a Halloween costume on, especially in this town."

"Touché. Just remember to order my pad Thai medium spicy. Do not fuck with me, Iris: Medium. Spicy."

"I would never," I say as I open the car door. "Except for that one time where I accidentally ordered extra spicy."

In my defense, I thought she could handle it. I never expected she'd be in the bathroom all night with a bottle of Pepto Bismol, asking me to come check if actual flames were coming out of her asshole. That was my bad.

"Oh, and Iris?" she says before I close the door.

I stop and lean into the car.

"Try and avoid the woman whose husband you just murdered."

I salute her. "I'll do my best."

I attempt to change my usual stride in hopes that the women won't recognize me. I can picture Lucy in the car, losing her mind laughing because she knows exactly what I'm trying to do. It somehow turns into an awkward limp, so I abandon the plan once I'm opening the door to the restaurant.

As I'd hoped, the women don't even stop their conversation when I walk in. I'm greeted by the cashier, who thankfully isn't the normal woman who takes my order because she likes to yell, "Iris! My sweet Iris!" and this one doesn't appear to know or recognize me. I lean on the counter, place my order, pay and tip in cash, and then sit in an empty booth to wait for my food. The women are two booths away and obviously think I'm a tourist because they don't lower the volume on their gossip session whatsoever.

"That old witch isn't going to say anything. She's been hiding in that apartment for almost forty years. If she was going to break, it would have already happened."

I think it was Brighton, but I can't be sure. They all sound the same. Stuck-up cunts with more money than sense. It's difficult to tell them apart when I don't have eyes on which set of injected lips are flapping. My first inclination is to think they are talking about Willow Nora, but I don't want to jump to conclusions. She would be none too pleased to hear that I assumed a conversation was about her because I heard the words "old witch."

"Bucky hasn't increased her rent since the nineties. She gets to live a quiet life selling weird shit and pretending she's psychic. She's content. She had nothing to do with Kellen's death, I promise you, ladies."

Well shit, I guess they are talking about Willow. I'm not sure I even knew Bucky owned her building, but it makes sense; he owns most of the town. For the record, my mother and I own the café and the property it's on, and we'd never sell to that asshole.

I'm not sorry Kellen is dead, but I hate that anyone considered Willow could be responsible, even for a minute. Hasn't this town put her through enough? I wonder what these miserable women are going on about. What do they want Willow to stay quiet about?

"Poor Barrett has barely been able to eat or sleep; he's so distraught over Kellen."

Well, lady, poor Barrett is dead now, so I guess we can cross his well-being off the prayer list.

"I do think we should organize some sort of vigil for Ann. The optics won't be great if we ignore it. We can look at the schedule tomorrow and pick a date. Make sure we can get the local news crew and the Westridge Gazette down to cover it. Did she have a favorite color? Ask one of her useless little boutique employees. We'll all wear whatever color it is and talk about how special it is to honor her life. We just can't do it on the thirtieth or it will coincide with the other fucking memorial, as if this town doesn't have enough of those. Can't interfere with a public in mourning, or they'll call us bitches even more than they already do."

They all cackle and clink their glasses together.

Wouldn't want to interfere with the memorial on the thirtieth, ladies? That's the anniversary of the worst day of my life, and this year, I'll be doing my best to make sure it's yours, as well.

Chapter Thirty-Seven

PRESENT DAY

Last night, Kayla's haunted corn maze opened to the public for its annual run. She texted me this morning to thank me again for helping her set up. They had the best opening night turnout ever, with over four hundred paying customers making their way through the one-acre maze. Not a single one of them detected an actual dead body among the dummies. He doesn't have a wife or kids, but I thought surely his mother or his employer would have noticed he was missing by now. My curiosity is getting the best of me; I've got to see this for myself.

As I'm getting ready for work, I yell out to Lucy, who is in the kitchen. "Lucy Goosey, want to go to the corn maze tonight?"

She stops what she's doing and comes to the door of the bathroom, where I'm pulling my hair up into a bun that will fit under my ninja mask. She crosses her arms and leans on the door frame, squinting her eyes at me.

"Why do you want to go to the corn maze, Iris?"

"Next week is Halloween. Can't a girl want to do something spooky? Plus, we need to support Kayla. Remember when you pushed her into Jessie Cantrell's pool with her clothes on in eighth grade? You owe her."

I can see movement from her direction, but I don't give her the satisfaction of turning my head to see her eyes roll.

"Oh yes, I definitely need to apologize for something I did when I was thirteen years old. Let's go to the maze."

"Okay," I say, ignoring her sarcastic tone. "I'll be off work by seven. Let's meet here and we can ride together."

"Okay, Iris. Let's do that."

She comes in even heavier with the sarcasm, but I've mastered the art of pretending I don't notice.

Sure, Lucy is the only friend I'd say I'm close to these days, but can you blame me? Not only is she the only one who gets me, like really gets me, but she's also one of my only friends who doesn't have kids. The rest of the girls that I spent time with during my twenties married their high school sweethearts, are knee-deep in after-school activities, and aren't capable of having conversations about anything other than potty training or the benefits of limiting screen time. They're all suddenly allergic to gluten, obsessed with the G-rated humor of Nate Bargaze, and require me to schedule coffee dates with them two months in advance. I'm over it. Lucy is all I need, and Wally is a welcome addition to my little circle.

I turn on a local radio station in the car for my short drive to work, and I'm shocked to hear the host speaking with Halloween Harrison, that dreadful podcaster who is in town to cover the murders. My heart stops when I hear mention of my name.

"Of course, Iris Thornwick and Wally Parker were there the night in question. The sisters were hired to babysit

Jack and Barrett Carter, and Kellen and Logan DeYoung. Ann Haven stopped by for at least a few hours during the night. That's seven witnesses, two of which are now dead. Why now? Why this year? This is not a significant anniversary, so why did Ann choose now to confess that she lied all those years ago? We know Iris and Wally won't be giving any statements, but we can't get ahold of Jack, Barrett, or Logan either. Rumors have swirled over the years that they regret the accusations they made as children, but they've never gone on the record to recant their statements. Will they, now that the witnesses seem to be targeted by someone in Westridge Cove? There are so many details to this case and everything that's happened over the years; I could stay in Westridge for months covering the crimes and I still wouldn't have time to investigate it all."

"And we haven't even mentioned the upcoming memorial on the thirtieth. I checked with the mayor's office, and there's no indication that the event will be cancelled due to the recent tragedies. It's Westridge Cove, after all; murder is just business as usual," says the host, giving their two cents.

"We haven't even mentioned Willow Nora; has anyone heard from her this month? Do we know she's alive and well?"

The radio host pushes a button that plays the chorus from *Witchy Woman* by the Eagles. If I wasn't due at work, I'd take a detour to the studio and knock his teeth out.

"That's a great question, Harrison. Westridge Covers, have *you* seen the elusive Widow Nora this month? Has she cast any spells on you? Call into the station and let us know."

I turn my radio off. *Idiots.*

As soon as I walk into the back door of the restaurant, I hurry to the manager's office to call Willow. I nearly called her on my cell but didn't feel like getting a lecture about who could be listening.

"This must be a Thornwick," she says as a greeting.

"Lucky for you, it's the good-looking one," I reply, trying to lighten the mood before I tell her the local radio station is fishing for information about her whereabouts.

"Ahh, Nancy," she says, and I can hear the pleasure in her voice. She waits a beat for me to protest, but when I don't fall into her trap, she continues. "Okay, Iris. To what do I owe the pleasure?"

"I was listening to Mikey in the Morning on my way in, and he's asking people to call the station if they've seen you this month. I guess with all the renewed attention to the case, they need to know every last detail about what all of us are up to. I just wanted to give you a heads up so maybe you can hide out more than usual until October is over."

She hesitates for a minute, and I'm concerned that I've upset her.

"My dear, you worry about me too much. My crystals are charged, my salt circle is formed; I am perfectly fine. This will all blow over."

"For someone who insists she's not a witch, you sure do a lot of witchy shit," I tell her while nodding to greet my mom who has walked into the office.

"You don't need to be a witch, you just need to have a few old remedies in your back pocket for situations such as this," she tells me.

"Hey, speaking of being a witch, you didn't happen to cast a spell on Wally and me, did you? We seem to be quite fond of each other lately, and it's a little fishy if you ask me."

Mom throws her head back laughing at the same time Willow barks out a laugh over the phone. It's so loud I have to pull the receiver away from my ear. Making either of them laugh feels like winning the lottery; making both of them laugh at the same time will give me joy for days.

"If there was a spell to make you two drop the act and admit you're in love, I think the people of this town would have done it years ago, because we're all sick and tired of watching you dance around it. Glad you both got on with it already."

I give her a light cussing before ending the call and turn to face Mom, who is blowing on her coffee and looking over the employee schedule for the day so she can draw out server sections.

"Maybe next year we find someone capable of running this place so we can go to the beach during October. What do you say?" I ask her.

"That would be nice, sweetie," she tells me in a tone that says she'd never dream of letting someone else run this restaurant.

The day is as uneventful as an October afternoon can be. Once again, we have more business than we know what to do with, but it's the last week in October, and there isn't an employee on the schedule who isn't used to it by now. Mom and I are both scheduled to leave around seven; we are trusting one of our shift managers to close the place up after the dinner rush. She was only reminded about thirty-six times that we are only a phone call and a short drive away if she needs anything.

As the clock nears seven, I begin moving Mom out the back door and into her car. Naturally, she starts to refuse and lists the many reasons why she should just stay and help for a few more hours.

"Mom, if you're burnt out, you're no help to anyone around here. Go home, take a hot bath, watch Dateline, and maybe treat yourself to one of those nice little Costco-brand sleeping pills so you can get a good eight hours."

She huffs with the dedication of a toddler who is told to go take a nap.

"Fine, but there's not even a new episode on until Friday, so I guess I'll have to watch something on Netflix."

"I cannot imagine how hard that must be for you. I'll be sending you my thoughts and prayers while you navigate this difficult situation," I say, handing over her purse and jacket from the back of the chair in the office.

"I don't know who you get that smart mouth from," she says, grabbing both items from me in such a dramatic motion, it makes me laugh out loud.

"I love you, mom."

"I love you too, my little flower."

It doesn't take much time to get ready for Kayla's maze because I'm already in a good enough costume to protect my identity. I'm dressed as a ninja, but Lucy keeps calling me *Beverly Hills Ninja*, and I believe there's an insult in there somewhere but I'm too exhausted to care.

I pull up to the gate and hand the entrance fee to Kayla's brother, Ben, and I catch a break when he doesn't notice my car in the dark. He's also dealing with a line out to the main road to get in, so I'm sure he's not even paying attention to what anyone is driving. He gives me my change, and I nod wordlessly before pulling through and finding a spot.

It's a perfect night for the maze—a little hazy, no wind, and warm enough to not need a winter coat. From where we are parked, it looks like the moon is hung directly above the rows of corn. Together with the fog, it looks like the poster for a horror movie.

"Ready?" I ask Lucy, my voice slightly muffled by the mask.

"Ready," she confirms.

We wait at the entrance to the maze until the worker, who just happens to be the son of a guy we graduated school with, listens to the screams of the group before us so he can gauge how far away they are before waving us in.

"You may proceed," he says in his best vampire voice, complete with plastic teeth impeding his speech. He lifts an arm, causing his black robe to flutter in the wind, as he directs us to go in.

Lucy grabs my arm and leans in to whisper, "Did you want to tell him about how you gave his dad a hand job while you were watching *Pet Sematary* sophomore year? Who even does that during a scary movie? You've been fucked up for a while, Iris."

"Will you shut the fuck up," I whisper back.

My heart rate increases at each dark turn as we go deeper through the path carved into the corn field. It's not because of the teenagers with chainsaws (I didn't expect them to be real; that actually did shock me), or the laughing clowns, or even the evil leprechaun that shoots out of a hiding spot and nearly makes me pee my pants.

"You won't be getting me gold!" he shouts as we hurry by.

I'm prepared to arrive at the scene and see Barrett's body, leaned up against a cross made of wood and corn stalks, next to two dummies in the same position. I'm not sure if I'd describe it as a high, but there's a certain level of excitement knowing that hundreds of tourists have walked this path in the last twenty-four hours and have no idea they were looking at an actual body. They might need therapy when the news breaks.

Finally, we arrive at the corner, just before the final scene. The memory comes to me in flashes—putting my disgust aside so I could convince Barrett I was flirting with him, offering him a drink from my flask, waiting for the drugs to kick in, strangling him with a wire, and then using that same wire to string him up. I'd never been so out of breath. I considered leaving him lying in the corn after the third time his body fell forward against mine as I attempted to lift the cross. Luckily, I persevered by propping it up against a piece of farm equipment, and even had a moment to admire my handiwork before leaving.

I inhale deeply before the crosses come into view.

Suddenly, I can't breathe.

"What the hell is wrong with you?" Lucy asks. "You look like you've seen an actual ghost. This is all fake, remember?"

Yes, I know it's all fake. Except for the one scene that is very real and includes the dead body of Barrett Carter in a recreation of one of my favorite scenes from one of my favorite scary movies. Fake body, real body, fake body. That's the scene I created.

But what I'm looking at is an empty cross. Barrett's body is gone.

Chapter Thirty-Eight

PRESENT DAY

Boy, am I in a pickle.

It's now been days since Lucy and I went through the maze, only to find no body where there absolutely should have been a body. Barrett Carter was officially reported missing after he failed to show up for several consecutive days of work, and his mother, using her spare key to her precious son's house, found it empty. Great, so the police department (led by my Wally) finds out that he was supposed to be volunteering at the haunted maze. They search the maze, they find his body, which has somehow fallen from the cross because I didn't secure him as tightly as I thought I did, right? *Wrong.* Barrett Carter's body is nowhere to be found. The maze has been searched, innocently confirmed by Wally this morning, who had no idea he was giving valuable information to the guilty party.

"Tell me what condition you left him in," Lucy says as I'm pacing in our living room after watching the local news coverage of his disappearance and stressing over the fact that Wally hasn't returned my texts in hours.

"Dead, Lucy. Dead is the condition I left him in."

"If you want me to help you, you're going to have to give me more information than that."

I replay the murder in my head, trying to think of anything I haven't already told Lucy.

"Oh," I say, remembering a lost detail. "I made a little crown and put it around his forehead like they did to Linda Hamilton in the movie."

You know that famous picture of Ben Affleck, smoking a cigarette and looking exhausted? Well, that's how Lucy looks right now. Minus the cigarette.

"What a nice touch, Iris," she says, dripping in sarcasm. "And you used gloves, right?"

I tut. "Of course I used gloves. I think we've only watched two hundred episodes of *Forensic Files* by now."

"And you're sure there's no way he survived?"

"Lucy, what do you want me to say? He was dead, I'm sure of it. It was total dead weight while I was trying to attach him to that stupid thing and get it to stand up, and I checked his pulse like a dozen times. Dead with a capital *D*."

"What are people saying online?"

"You don't want to know," I tell her. I stayed up entirely too late once the news broke of his disappearance so I could see what they were posting on social media; I had to see the theories. She cocks her head at my response, so I tell her. "Okay, okay. They think he's the killer. They think he killed Kellen and made a run for it."

"Iris, I can see your lip twitching. You're fighting a smile. How perfect for you that there are now four murders, including the Burntwood Burglar, none of which you are a suspect in."

"Lucy, I didn't kill Ann, and that douchebag in Burntwood leapt to his death, remember? Hey, speaking of Ann, I meant to ask you, why are there sleeping pills in the bathroom cabinet?"

Her eyes fall to the floor. "Iris, I think you know why they are in there."

No, actually Lucy, I don't. But I'm stressed about this whole missing body situation, and I don't feel like arguing with you, so I'm going to keep my mouth shut.

We sit in silence, focusing on the TV, as Sophia Smith interviews Bucky Lancaster in front of an office building that houses Lancaster Enterprises.

"Mayor Lancaster, Barrett Carter is the second employee of yours to go missing this month. Kellen DeYoung's body was found, and the cause of death was ruled homicide. Now Barrett hasn't been seen in days. Are you concerned that your employees are being targeted?"

"Great question, Sophia," Bucky says with his sideways smile and subtle wink that comes off like a car salesman from 1980. "Rather than focusing on the connection of these young men working for Lancaster Enterprises, I'd be more concerned about their connection to the Thornwick case. There are thousands of tourists in our little town this month, and we know how intense some of these true-crime sleuths can be. I certainly hope that Westridge Cove Public Safety is focusing on that angle while they conduct their investigation."

I pick up the remote and click the power button to shut it off.

"Wow, now he's got the town wondering if a tourist could have killed them. The online forums are thinking

Barrett is guilty and on the run. The real housewives of Westridge Cove have their eyes on Willow Nora. It sounds like you're just getting off scot-free here, aren't you, Iris?"

I'm not sure what she's so mad at me for. We were supposed to be in this together.

Chapter Thirty-Nine

PRESENT DAY

Here we are, October thirtieth. The day I've been dreading. There had to be something I could do to counteract the all-consuming grief this day would surely bring, so I planned my final act of revenge, and it's going to be a big one.

Mom and I work our early shifts at the café, with the employees tiptoeing around us as if we're made of glass and the customers none the wiser since we're in costume. By now, most people know how to act when their friends, loved ones, or coworkers experience grief. You tell them you're thinking of them or praying for them or whatever the hell you believe in, offer some comforting words, and then do something to make their life easier like baking a casserole they can heat up when they're hungry. The issue with this loss is that it's so great and tragic, nobody really knows how to act around us.

"Do you want to ride together?" Mom asks as we are gathering our things after the first dinner rush. We're once again trusting a shift manager to close down the restaurant, but neither of us have the energy to be concerned about it. We leave through the back door without so much as reminding her that we're only a phone call away. We're going to stand in forty-degree weather and listen to people say kind words about a situation that doesn't warrant any.

"I'm going to stop home and do a few things. Do you mind if I meet you there?" I ask.

"Sure, sweetie. I'm going to pick up Willow on my way. She said she'd like to come."

This surprises me, but Willow tends to show up when it really matters. I'm glad she's coming. She can keep Mom company in my absence.

"Bucky said the Westridge Cove High School choir is going to sing a few songs. I think that will be nice."

Yes, Mom, it will be a nice soundtrack to play while thousands of gawkers watch us relive the worst day of our lives.

"I agree. Why don't you and Willow save me a spot near the front and I'll meet you there?"

"Okay, sweetie. You're sure you're okay on your own?"

What I'm doing is best done alone, I want to tell her, but instead I just smile and nod.

"Tomb Raider? You know, it's not too late. You don't have to do this," Lucy tells me as I lace up my black boots in front of the full-length mirror in my bedroom.

"I'm not dressed as Tomb Raider. She wore shorts. This is just a tactical outfit. You've made it very clear that you're not coming along for this one, so why don't you stay out of my business?"

The words hurt me more than they hurt her, but they needed to be said. I need to be by myself for this one.

"You need to be at the memorial, Iris. You will regret it if you don't go."

"You sound like my mother," I respond, tucking a hunting knife into the strap around my thigh. I may be a few inches shorter and twenty pounds heavier, but I would give Angelina Jolie a run for her money. I have four weapons strapped to me and a plan A, B, and C. I'm out for revenge, and I'm prepared.

"And your mother is going to wonder why you aren't there."

"Everyone in this town will be there. Every tourist will be there, hoping for a glimpse of one of us. The news station will be there, the radio hosts, and even the fucking podcasters. But you know who will leave immediately after giving his remarks? Butthole Bucky. Because he can't stand to be away from the office for one fucking night so he can refresh the sales pages of all his businesses and count his money like Scrooge McDuck while his secretary is on her knees, performing her after-hours duty. I know exactly what time she leaves to make it home to her own husband, so while everyone else is in mourning, listening to the choir sing "Amazing Grace," I'll be delivering karma directly to that man's mahogany desk."

Lucy slams her hand on the door frame to convey her displeasure in my plan.

"Iris, you have no proof that Bucky Lancaster was involved at all. Don't you think proof would be a good thing to have before you fucking kill a man?"

"Lucy, he was there. That's all the proof I need. Now, if you'll excuse me, I've got work to do."

Chapter Forty

PRESENT DAY

Main Street is empty, just as I expected. My gun is loaded, taser is holstered, and both knives are strapped tight. I've played through this scenario a hundred times, and a chill goes down my spine when I realize it's finally happening. This is it.

I have Sarah's Walkman clipped to my waistband, and after looking around once more to make sure I'm alone, I put the headphones over my ears and press play.

The first song on her mixed tape is "(Don't Fear) The Reaper," which is what I always envisioned I'd play as the soundtrack for my revenge killing tonight. Something about it doesn't feel quite right, so I fast forward.

"Psycho Killer." Nope, too on the nose.

"Friday I'm in Love." Not today, the Cure.

Finally, I fast forward until I hear the opening notes of a song that I know will be perfect. The beat of the drums gives me goosebumps. This is it.

"Burning Down the House."

I smile and begin my five-block walk down the alley behind Main Street, the exact path my aunts took before they disappeared. Although nobody seems to know where they were headed or what their mission was, mine is clear: Kill Bucky Lancaster.

The sun has now completely set, and the street is lit only by the orange twinkling lights strung from the lamp-posts and the moon, which is set in the sky in a way that makes me feel like it's sitting front row for the show I'm about to put on.

I'm walking down the center of the alley, and there's still nobody in sight. It's a ghost town. I'm still not entirely sure I'm going to pull this off and get away with it, so I enjoy what I understand may be my last moments of freedom.

I'm on my way to commit premeditated murder of a man I've known my entire life and, heaven help me, I begin to dance.

As David Byrne warns of nasty weather, I'm kicking my feet out with the rhythm.

I hop to the side and do a little shake as he promises to fight fire with fire.

I might just dance all the way to Bucky's office door and shoot him between the eyes before the song is even over.

After tonight, all will be right in the world. Justice will be served. If I make it out alive, I'll play this song again tomorrow morning as I'm eating my eggs and toast.

I nearly jump out of my skin when a hand grabs my shoulders. I throw my headphones off, and they land in the street, just as they did when Sarah lost them all those years ago.

"Iris."

"Wally," I respond with short, haggard breaths.

"You don't have to do this."

"Do what?" I say, as if I don't look like an armed assassin ready for a fight.

"Kill another person because of what you think they're responsible for."

The word *another* stops me in my tracks. Does he know? His eyes are pleading with me to change my mind.

"1993 was a long time ago, Iris. We were kids. You can't kill people for what we did as kids. Logan DeYoung and Jack Carter—is that who you're after tonight? The last two people involved with what happened to your aunts? They're at the memorial. Where you should be."

"Logan and Jack? Because they accused my aunts of being witches when they were six years old? Wally, that's what you think this is about?"

"I had a hunch you had something to do with Kellen. I've been doing this job a long time and there was something about your lack of remorse that got my mind spinning. I went to the maze after you mentioned that you helped set it up because I knew Barrett would be there and I had a horrible feeling. That's when I found him. This has to stop, Iris."

"You found Barrett? You moved his body?" I gasp.

"Of course I did, Iris. I love you. I'd do anything for you. But this has to stop; we were just kids," he repeats again. "They didn't know any better."

This may be only the second time I've seen him cry. The first was a year ago tonight, after he found his father on the ground, unconscious.

"Wally, look at me. This has nothing to do with what happened to my aunts. This has nothing to do with Logan and Jack; they have no part of this. I know they were just kids. They were just doing what their parents told them to do, and I don't blame them. Logan and Jack grew up to be great men. I killed Kellen and Barrett because of what they did to your dad . . . and what they did to Lucy."

Chapter Forty-One

ONE YEAR AGO

"Lucy, we do a lot of stupid things, but fucking married men isn't one of them. Especially a married man who is your boss."

She collapsed on the couch, rolling her eyes.

"I should have never told you."

"No, I'm your best friend," I reminded her. "You should tell me everything, but it's also my job to be truthful with you. So here I am, telling you this is a bad idea."

"He's not going to be married for long. Kellen told me that he and Callie have been having issues for years."

I threw up my hands in defeat.

"They all say that, Lucy! You cannot be this stupid."

She sat back up, slid her feet into her black heels, and grabbed her bag.

"Since you love to track my location, there's no use lying to you. I'm going to Kellen's cabin to watch the Bucks game with him and Barrett. He makes me happy. I really wish you'd give him a chance."

"Give him a chance, Luce? I've known him longer than you have. He's an asshole. He cheats on his wife, he's your boss, and none of this is okay. What would Bucky say if he found out that one of his right-hand men is fucking one of his newest employees?"

"Bucky knows about it. He said he might even stop by tonight while I'm there."

That was my breaking point.

"Lucy, it's like I don't even know you."

With that, she shook her head and stormed out of the apartment while I fumed. She barely acknowledged the anniversary of my aunts' disappearance that day. Normally we'd spend it together. Devil's Night; it was a tradition. Now she was choosing Kellen Fucking DeYoung over me. I should have told her the stories about him from high school —how I met two girls from Burntwood at a cheerleading competition who told me he got forceful with them the year before. He was not a good man.

My sulking was interrupted by the buzz of my phone on the coffee table, and it took me a moment to register Willow's phone number. She never called me on my cell, but I knew her number by heart because I dialed it from the café phone often.

"Willow?"

"Iris, where is Lucy?"

"Headed out to spend time with . . . a friend. Why?"

"I just had the most vivid premonition. I haven't had one like this since your aunts disappeared. Iris, Lucy is in danger. Wherever she is, you have to stop her. Tell her to come back home."

I can't explain why, but I didn't doubt her for a minute. I'd known Willow my entire life, and she'd never given me a warning like this. Without a second thought, I called Rex Parker immediately after ending my call with Willow.

I'll never forget the night at the Alibi when I was finally old enough to drink and shared a night on the town with my mom and Rex. After a few whiskey sours, he began to talk about that day in 1993.

"She knew things, Iris. You know I don't believe in all that hibbity dibbity, but she just knew things. I'd never admit it to the guys, but I've dropped by Willow's apartment a few times when I've been stuck on a case. She's usually quite helpful. She's batshit crazy, sure, but she's also quite helpful."

I knew he'd listen to me if I called.

"Iris, you doing okay?" he said, answering his cell on the first ring.

"Rex, it's about Lucy. I know you're going to think I'm crazy, but Willow thinks she's in danger. She's headed out to Kellen DeYoung's cabin on County Road 820. Do you think you can check on her?"

Within a minute, I could hear his keys turning the ignition in the background. He wasn't wasting any time.

"Iris, I don't think you're crazy in the least. If Willow Nora says Lucy is in danger, I can assure you that it's at least worth looking into."

"Thank you, Rex. Okay, hold on. I'm tracking her location. It looks like she's pulled over by the river next to the boat launch on the north side of town. I don't know why. How far away are you?"

"Not far at all, Iris. I'll check it out and call you back. If she moves, let me know."

"Okay, Rex. Thank you."

The thing is—I knew. I just knew something bad was going to happen while I waited for Rex's call. I felt it so deep in my stomach, it was like the sense of doom was imbedded in my organs. I just pictured poor Lucy, trying to impress Kellen's stupid ass while he and Barrett got drunk and took things too far with her. Why the fuck did I let her leave the apartment?

It took twenty-two minutes before I received the call, and those were the longest minutes of my life. Twenty-two minutes, and my life was changed forever.

Chapter Forty-Two

"What makes you think they killed Lucy?" Wally asks me.

"She was having an affair with Kellen, Wally. She was on her way to go see him and Barrett that night."

"Why wouldn't you tell me that, Iris? You didn't have to kill them; I could have investigated them. Bucky confirmed that all of his employees had alibis that night; they were all accounted for. Are you sure about this?"

I try not to scream in frustration. Why is it always such a shock to men that other men can be lying to their faces?

"Of course Bucky would say that. He was planning to meet up with them. He knew. Why would he lie about their alibis if he wasn't at least a little suspicious that Kellen and Barrett killed her? Hell, maybe he was already there, too!"

"And my dad just happened upon the three of them? Are you saying that Barrett or Kellen hit my dad over the head with that tire iron?"

This. This is the secret I haven't told anyone.

"I called your dad that night, Wally. I'm the reason he almost died. I'm the reason he was there."

"What? No, he was responding to a call of a drunk driver by the river. That's why he was out there."

I slowly shake my head.

"It was me, Wally. Once he started to recover, and his memory from that night was lost, that's when I decided I'd have to take matters into my own hands. I needed to make these assholes pay for what they did to Lucy and your dad. You were too preoccupied with caring for him to follow any leads I'd give you, and Bucky had already lied about their alibis. I knew I'd have to prove it myself and kill them. They took my best friend, Wally, and they could have taken Rex, too."

He's staring straight ahead rather than at me. I wish I knew what thoughts are running through his head: Is he going to turn me in? Will he forgive me? Can we ever have a relationship after this? I'm the reason his father almost died.

"For an entire year, I've been hoping that Dad's memory of that night would come back so he could tell me who did this to him. To Lucy," Wally says, maintaining eye contact with the asphalt before him.

"So have I," I respond, and it's the truth. For the first few months, I visited Rex in the hospital, and then at his house, and finally at the assisted living home. I tried everything I could think of to jog his memory, to try and bring the events of that night back to him. Nothing worked. He was a shell of a man, and it was all my fault.

"Forget about Bucky tonight, Iris. We'll handle him later. Put the gun back in your car and let's go to the memorial. Tonight's about honoring Lucy."

"I was trying to honor her by killing that asshole," I

mutter under my breath as we walk back to my car. Wally's eyebrows raise in shock as I unload all of the weapons I had strapped to my body. "Fine, let's go. I've got a change of clothes in my backseat."

The three-block trek to Lucy's memorial feels like someone else's body is taking me through the motions. I refuse to believe that she's gone. I don't know that I can do this.

When I see Mom and Willow in the front row, my knees nearly give out. I hear whispers, pointed fingers, and snaps of cameras as the crowd begins to notice my arrival. Mom and Willow ignore them all and hold out their hands to welcome me.

A picture of Lucy is projected on a giant screen next to the fountain, where her foster sister is speaking. It's a picture from two summers ago when we went to New England. She has a bib on and a crab leg in each hand. It was the trip of a lifetime, and we joked about moving there so many times, it nearly became an actual plan.

"Lucy and I both came from rough backgrounds. We were unwanted kids who had never experienced uncondi-tional love. That is, of course, before the Thornwicks took her in and made her part of a real family for the first time in her life. From seventh grade until the day she died, Lucy's life was changed because Nancy and Iris Thornwick loved her so much, she nearly forgot she'd ever been without it. So, Nancy and Iris, after a lifetime of pain from your own personal tragedies, you showed my foster sister the kind of love we all dream of, and for that, I'm so thankful to you. Now," she said, turning her attention to the vast crowd, "someone here has to know something. It's been a full year without answers about what happened to Lucy Edwards.

This will be the year we bring her killers to justice. I'm sure of it."

"Someone should tell her you already did," Lucy whispers in my ear.

I look at her and wipe a tear away, shaking my head. When she sees the expression on my face, she knows it's time to go, and her image starts fading away.

"It's for the best, Iris. You've got to let me go. Live your life. I'll always be watching."

She floats, which is how I like to picture her in the afterlife. Her body ascends into the night sky until I can't feel her presence anymore, but I somehow know she's still watching.

"What are you looking at, sweetie?" my mom asks, reaching a hand up to rub my back.

"Nothing, Mom. I was just thinking about how lucky we were to know her."

Chapter Forty-Three

OCTOBER 30ᵀᴴ, 1993

"Are you sure we don't look ridiculous?" Bridget asked, straightening out her black pointed hat.

"It's Halloween; we're supposed to look ridiculous," Sarah assured her.

"Dolly Parton says that if you can't make fun of yourself, why bother," Maggie chimed in while putting her own hat on. "This town has been asking for witches, and witches is what they'll get."

They are gathered in the alley behind Willow's Nook, dressed in the costumes their mother, Sheila, handmade them the week before. Black robes, black hats, adhesive warts, and cheap plastic brooms. The full look.

"Everyone have their Walkmans cued up?" Sarah asks.

The girls nod their heads.

"Let's practice this once before we take our parade to Main Street."

Sarah motions for them to put their headphones on and press play.

"(Don't Fear) The Reaper" begins playing at a low volume in unison from each of their cassette tapes.

They each let out the most chilling cackle they can muster, before skipping over the small gravel rocks of the alley and holding hands.

"Look out, Westridge Cove! We're here to take your children," Maggie calls out.

"We only need a few of them to complete our ritual," Bridget adds.

Maggie and Bridget are jerked backward when Sarah, who is in the middle, suddenly pulls on both of their arms. The girls spin to see why their sister has stopped, just in time to see her headphones flying through the air and landing on the sidewalk beside Willow's building, her cassette player bouncing to a stop next to them.

"What the hell?" Sarah says, hands instinctively going to her ears, where her headphones were just violently ripped off. "What are you doing here?"

"What the fuck is this about?" Maggie asks, just two seconds before everything goes black.

Chapter Forty-Four

"She's been with you, yeah?" Willow asks before setting a mug of tea in front of me at the table. She takes a spoon and stirs her own before taking the seat opposite me.

I nod and hang my head, not quite sure why I'm ashamed. I've been living with Lucy's ghost for a full year, pretending she's going to work, watching movies together, plotting the deaths of the men who killed her while she watched. I nearly lose my composure when I think of the sedatives the doctor prescribed me when I was inconsolable after her body was found. Lucy had been strangled and left next to the river like trash. I'd torn the label off and convinced myself I didn't know why they were in my bathroom. It's amazing the lies your mind will begin to believe when you repeat them enough.

"I've known you had something special since you were a little kid, Iris. You've got a great intuition, and I think you've sensed things before they've happened; you just didn't know how to explain the feeling you experience, deep inside."

"Hallucinating my dead best friend for the last year doesn't make me special, Willow. It makes me insane."

She shakes her head and gives me a weak smile.

"You're not insane, dear. This town has always had a thin veil between the living and the dead. It's just hard to talk about it out loud, or people will think you're nuts," she says, with a comical shrug.

"Willow . . . Kellen and Barrett killed Lucy. I'm sure of it."

She places a hand over mine. "I know, dear."

"You know? Why didn't you tell me?" I ask.

"Because my intuition told me you were handling the situation."

"And why didn't you tell Wally?"

Her lips tighten as she considers her words. "I suppose for the same reason you didn't. I wasn't sure how I was going to convince him of their guilt without any evidence. Wally and I get along fine, but he doesn't trust my visions like his father did."

"I tried to gather the evidence myself, Willow. Did you know that asshole used a burner phone when he talked to Lucy? His real cell phone was sitting at the office. They didn't even drive his car, which had GPS . . . I think they took their Polaris out there, but I can't prove it. I just don't understand why—why they had to kill her. Were they just that worried she'd tell Kellen's wife? Was that worth killing Lucy over? Or were they just sick fucks who got off on killing?"

I sit with my anger for a moment before deciding to let Willow know the information that has changed everything.

"He knows, Willow. He knows I killed them. He's not going to arrest me."

"I know, dear; I made sure his love for you was stronger than his conscience."

I knew it. She did this. She made him fall in love with me. How could she?

"Calm down, Iris. He was already in love with you. I just used a few tricks I had up my sleeve to compromise his sense of moral obligations to the law on this one because I saw where it was headed if I didn't."

"What do I do now?" I ask, feeling so mentally exhausted I'm not even sure I'm ready to hear a plan for moving forward. "I still haven't confronted Bucky about his involvement, and I'm not sure I can sleep until he pays for what he's done."

"Oh, dear," Willow says, moving her chair closer to mine. "First, I think it's probably time we talk about the real Witches of Westridge."

My mind immediately goes to Lancaster. DeYoung. Carter. The *bitches* of Westridge.

"What do they have against you, anyway? If you know so much about them, why aren't you talking?"

It may be brief, but I catch it: Her eyes dart to the cherrywood urn sitting on the side table next to her couch.

I know, without a word, everything. Willow's right; there's something inside me that I don't yet know how to control or use to my advantage, but the answers are spelled out for me like someone is whispering them into my ear.

"You *did* kill your husband," I say.

Her eyes widen in a flash of panic, before settling with recognition. I'm just like her . . . She didn't realize how much until now.

"They know you killed your husband, and they are

holding it over your head, so you'll keep your mouth shut about the things they've done."

She hangs her head and nods.

"My aunts? Did they have something to do with my aunts, other than convincing the town that they were practicing witchcraft? Did they kill them, Willow? Did they kill Ann?"

This time she holds both of my hands in hers. The look on her face tells me she can't believe she's finally going to come clean after all these years.

"I figure Devil's Night is as good a night as any to blow the lid off this whole thing. I'm ready if you are."

A note from the author:

If you've read about the Salem Witch Trials, some names may have sounded familiar: Sarah, Bridget, and Margaret were the names of three of the victims and Ann, the person who falsely accused them of witchcraft and later recanted and apologized for her lies.

I visited Salem for the first time last year and while touring the town and soaking in its tragic history, something stuck in my mind: they weren't witches, they were just people. They were simply innocent people who lost their lives over false accusations and now we all flock to their beautiful town every year to celebrate Halloween. That's when I started developing the idea for this book.

The other major inspiration for Witches of Westridge was the satanic panic, particularly the McMartin Preschool and West Memphis Three cases, which both fascinated me. If you'd like to learn more about these cases, or the satanic panic in general, I'd recommend the following:

Movie: Indictment: The McMartin Trial
Movie: West of Memphis

Book: Unmask Alice: LSD, Satanic Panic, and the Imposter Behind the World's Most Notorious Diaries by Rick Emerson

Acknowledgments

I don't think I've ever been so excited about writing book two; I started outlining it the minute this one was finished! Thank you to my beta readers and ARC readers for acting so excited about the book—you're the reason I decided to release the entire series within a year. I can't wait to finish this story with you.

Thank you to my agent, Claire Harris, for always having my back and to Podium Entertainment for acquiring the audio rights; I can't wait to hear it.

To my editors, Erika and Carly, thank you for always making my books better and having such thoughtful suggestions.

My high school friends (the Toilet Paper Vixens from Delta County!) were kind enough to loan me their children's names for this book, despite some of them not making it out alive.

Thank you Brandon Kobs from Allsweet in OKC for designing the cover; I can't wait to see what you come up with for the rest of the series!

For my friends on social media: I call you friend because that's what you've become and through the turmoil I've experienced in the last few months, you solidified that status. Thank you for checking in and caring.

To all the book influencers I have been fortunate enough to "meet" online in the last few years: I cannot tell you what your kind words mean to me. Every single day you bring me new readers, many of whom become friends. Thank you for all that you do.

For my family, especially my big sister, thank you for always cheering me on and making me believe there's no way I could fail.

For the love of my life, Cash, who filled an entire white-board with notes and suggestions for this book, I'm sorry I wanted to strangle you, and I now acknowledge that the feedback was incredibly helpful. What would I do without you?

Finally, to the reader: thank you for reading my words. Thank you for telling your friends. Thank you for writing the reviews I'm too anxious to read and sending them to me because you know I won't read them on my own. Thank you for being kind, understanding, patient, and hyping my books when I don't have the energy to take on the task myself. I am so ridiculously lucky to have you in my corner.

I'll see you heathens in a few months for book two.

I love to hear from readers! Reach out anytime:
Email: info@jlhyde.com
Instagram: @bookandbeerreview
Facebook: Author JL Hyde
TikTok: AuthorJLHyde
Mail: PO Box 205
Gladstone, MI 49837